P9-DIF-066

He couldn't reach her quickly enough.

Hannah's body crumpled. She hit the hardwood in the hallway hard.

The house reeked of exhaust. Gabe's head pounded. He had to get Hannah into fresh air before both of them dropped and never got up again. There was no telling how long she'd been breathing in the odorless gas.

She was struggling to stand. "We have...to...get out."

"I know." Gabe reached down and hefted her to her feet. "Lean on me. We'll get out. You'll feel better outside."

"Open the windows."

Maybe he should have, but they needed to get out fast. He swept his hand behind Hannah's knees and cradled her in his arms.

She tucked her head against his shoulder and mumbled something indecipherable. She was fading fast. There was no telling how long the car had been running.

He made his way around the corner at the end of the hall and into the kitchen, Hannah growing heavier with each step. "Hang on for me. We're getting outside as fast as we can."

Only this time, there was no response...

Jodie Bailey writes novels about freedom and the heroes who fight for it. Her novel *Crossfire* won a 2015 RT Reviewers' Choice Best Book Award. She is convinced a camping trip to the beach with her family, a good cup of coffee and a great book can cure all ills. Jodie lives in North Carolina with her husband, her daughter and two dogs.

Books by Jodie Bailey

Love Inspired Suspense

Dead Run
Calculated Vendetta
Fatal Response
Mistaken Twin
Hidden Twin
Canyon Standoff
"Missing in the Wilderness"
Fatal Identity
Under Surveillance
Captured at Christmas
Witness in Peril
Blown Cover
Deadly Vengeance

Alaska K-9 Unit

Deadly Cargo

Rocky Mountain K-9 Unit

Defending from Danger

Visit the Author Profile page at LoveInspired.com.

DEADLY VENGEANCE

JODIE BAILEY

LOVE INSPIRED SUSPENSE
INSPIRATIONAL ROMANCE

If you purchased this book without a cover you should be aware that this book is stolen property. It was reported as "unsold and destroyed" to the publisher, and neither the author nor the publisher has received any payment for this "stripped book."

LOVE INSPIRED® SUSPENSE

INSPIRATIONAL ROMANCE

Recycling programs
for this product may
not exist in your area.

ISBN-13: 978-1-335-58760-2

Deadly Vengeance

Copyright © 2023 by Jodie Bailey

All rights reserved. No part of this book may be used or reproduced in any manner whatsoever without written permission except in the case of brief quotations embodied in critical articles and reviews.

This is a work of fiction. Names, characters, places and incidents are either the product of the author's imagination or are used fictitiously. Any resemblance to actual persons, living or dead, businesses, companies, events or locales is entirely coincidental.

For questions and comments about the quality of this book, please contact us at CustomerService@Harlequin.com.

Love Inspired
22 Adelaide St. West, 41st Floor
Toronto, Ontario M5H 4E3, Canada
www.LoveInspired.com

Printed in U.S.A.

For we are his workmanship, created in Christ Jesus unto good works, which God hath before ordained that we should walk in them.
—*Ephesians* 2:10

To Michell.

Without your help,
this book never would have survived the brain fog.

Thank you.

ONE

No way. Not even if they paid him a million dollars and threw in a year's worth of El Casa's famous chips and salsa.

Gabe Buchanan planted his feet on the tile floor and sat taller in the fake leather chair situated at a long conference table surrounded by a dozen identical chairs. How had he landed here? Some clandestine military investigative unit might want him to sign on as a civilian consultant, but they couldn't have him or his cyberpsychology skills.

Especially not if *she* was involved.

He stared at the digital presentation in the dark, windowless conference room on Camp McGee and pretended to read the words that discussed the yet-to-be identified unit. He let his gaze slide past the large monitor to the woman sitting at the far end of the table.

Her hair was pulled back in a short braid, the red so dark that it was nearly brown. Her face was thinner, and if he were honest, he had to admit her Army combat uniform fit her well. The years had been good to her.

But they hadn't been good enough to make him forget.

As though she could feel him watching, Chief Warrant Officer Hannah Austin glanced his way.

Gabe returned his gaze to the front of the room, where some colonel whose name he'd already forgotten touted the successes of a unit that didn't officially exist. One Gabe would never know full details about unless he signed on the dotted line.

He wouldn't. He'd known that before he arrived.

He resisted the urge to glance at his watch. Why had he even come?

Because Hannah had issued the invitation, and Gabe's curiosity had worked against him. Nine years had gone by, and he hadn't been able to deny himself the opportunity to see who she'd become.

Frankly, he'd also wanted to know why a classified military investigative unit would court someone like him. A guy who lived and breathed forensic psychology and digital sociology, studying people's online and off-line behavior to build comprehensive profiles used by hiring managers at companies around the world. Rather than profile from a crime backward, he profiled a person going forward, trying to predict their future actions. His work went deeper than background checks or interviews. It was—

The lights flipped on, and Gabe blinked against the brightness and hoped no one realized his mind was anywhere but in this room.

"Do you have any questions, Mr. Buchanan?" The colonel braced his fists on the table and waited.

Hannah gave the colonel her full attention. For someone who had reached out to Gabe personally, she hadn't said a word to him since he'd entered the room. Maybe seeing him for the first time in nine years had brought up some guilt in her. Maybe she—

"Mr. Buchanan? Questions?"

Great. He was drifting again. "Why me?" It was the first thing that popped into his head.

Hannah swung her chair to face him, her eyes wide.

"I'm sorry?" The colonel looked nearly as incredulous as Hannah.

Might as well go all in. "I'm a psychology nerd and a computer geek, sir. I have zero interest in packing a pistol and working hands-on during any criminal investigation." When Hannah leaned forward as though she was going to speak, he kept talking. "I like what I do. I look for liars and cheats and not-who-they-say-they-ares from behind a screen, not in the field. Thank you for the offer, but my answer is *no.*"

Before the colonel could respond, Hannah stood. "Sir, could I speak to Mr. Buchanan privately?"

Gabe nearly rolled his eyes. No, she could not. Not even if they threw in some guac with that year's worth of salsa. He had nothing to say to her.

So...why are you here again?

Gabe clamped the end of his tongue between his teeth, because the grad-student-turned-soldier who'd stomped his heart flat still haunted his dreams.

Maybe he wanted her to know he'd become successful. That he was fine without her.

You're thirty-three years old, bud. You should be past this.

Well, maybe he wasn't.

With a curt nod, the colonel rounded the table and left the room, closing the door behind him. That left Gabe to face the woman who'd sliced him in the heart nine years earlier.

He crossed his arms over his chest, hoping to project

more nonchalance than he felt, and leaned back slightly in the chair. "Why did you call me, ma'am?"

Yeah, he'd Googled how to address someone with her military rank. She winced at the formality. They'd been friends once. Could have been something more.

Pressing her lips together, she stared at the blank screen. Finally, she faced him. "I need you."

The words weren't meant to be intimate, but they caught Gabe in the heart, zinging him back to graduate school. He'd have given all he owned to hear her say that back then.

Instead, he'd watched her walk away from the friendship he'd thought was growing into *something*. She'd fallen straight into the arms of his roommate without looking back.

Now her declaration was from a strictly mercenary standpoint. "You don't need me." He glanced at the door to make sure it was shut, then laced his fingers on the table. "You don't even want me." Gabe fought a wince of his own. He wanted to crawl under his chair. Had he really just said that?

She looked as though he'd thrown a punch. "Gabe, what happened in grad school…? I'm sorry."

Boy, she was a good liar. He almost believed her.

She rounded the table, sat two chairs away and leaned toward him. "After what happened with Trevor, I wanted to reach out to you, but you'd made it clear you didn't want to talk to me."

He was pretty sure that went the other way around. After Trevor was arrested, and Gabe had needed a friend the most, Hannah had disappeared. "I'm not here to rehash history. What do you really want?"

He was ready to get out of here. Half of his day had been spent getting onto the post and then sitting through this meeting. He needed to get back to the office. He was in the middle of building profiles on the top contenders for the CFO position at Assurance Trust Financial, an investment firm out of Fargo, North Dakota.

"I want you on my team." Hannah held up a hand. "I don't need a run-of-the-mill field agent. I need someone who can look at a person's online behavior and their real-world actions and marry the two into a comprehensive profile. Guess their next move. Help us get a step ahead of them. Plenty of people can do that, but you do it better than any of them. You have a skill set that—"

"No." Flattery would get her nowhere. "I'm happy at Skylark Profiling. Thanks for the offer, but I own half the company. I can't leave." He stood and headed for the door. "There's no need to walk me out."

"Gabe." It was almost a plea.

He stopped with his hand on the door.

"This is important. I want to build an investigative team that can take down major players around the world. Dangerous people. Real-life bullies."

Bullies. His fingers tightened around the door handle. His early years had been marked by tormentors who'd harassed and degraded him. Hannah was aware of that. In those months they'd gotten to know each other, he'd opened up to her like no one else.

Yet she'd still left him behind as soon as Trevor turned his attention to her. Whether she'd meant to or not, she'd reinforced every awful thing he'd believed about himself since elementary school. *Loser. Second best. Never good enough.*

This had gone on for too long. "Goodbye, Hannah." Gabe walked out of the room and shut the door behind him.

He strode down the oatmeal-colored tiles of the hallway, head up, eyes on the glass exit doors. Let Hannah be the one to tell the colonel he wouldn't be signing on. He just wanted to get out of here and pretend he'd never come to this meeting.

Gabe stepped through the double doors and into the bright fall afternoon light. His gray SUV was in the center of the parking lot, and he headed up the sidewalk that bisected the building's expansive lawn. He never should have come. Seeing Hannah Austin after all these years brought up emotions about a season of his life that he'd rather forget.

He glanced both ways in the U-shaped drive that crossed in front of the military office complex and noted a big blue pickup idling in front of the next building over. He stepped onto the asphalt, focused on his SUV.

He'd grab coffee and get back—

On his left, tires screeched, and he whirled around.

The pickup roared toward him.

And a force slammed him to the ground.

Hannah tried to roll as she tackled Gabe onto the grass median between the driveway and the parking lot, but his elbow caught her in the ribs, forcing the air from her lungs. They grunted as their bodies hit the ground.

Her ears were ringing, but the sound of an engine accelerating away overrode the internal noise. Staggering to her knees, Hannah tried to read the license plate as the truck roared around the corner and raced away.

Looked like Iowa plates.

She snatched her beret from the ground and pivoted on her knees toward the seven or eight people who'd rushed out the door, picking out the specialist on duty. "Call the MPs. Have them be on the lookout for a blue Chevy, full-size pickup, Iowa plates. First three letters *HXS*. Alert the gates." Whoever was behind the wheel wouldn't get far. The MPs at Camp McGee would be certain they didn't get off post.

As the specialist raced inside, Hannah tugged her beret onto her head and turned to Gabe. He lay flat on his back, his dark hair mussed from the impact. With one hand resting on his stomach, he stared at the sky as he heaved in air.

She'd probably knocked the wind right out of him. "You okay?"

He narrowed his impressive blue eyes. "You tackle… like an… NFL…linebacker."

"Lots of practice. But I promise you'd rather get taken to the ground by me than by that truck."

As he sat up, it sounded like he muttered "guess again."

She hoped not, but it wouldn't surprise her if he had. From the icy chill in his expression during their meeting, he hadn't forgiven her for what he likely viewed as a betrayal. He wouldn't be wrong. While her actions had been necessary, they'd wounded Gabe, and she'd been too green back then to know how to handle the situation.

A situation she'd created by getting too close to him in the first place.

With his knees bent and his elbows resting on them, Gabe waved away the help offered by several soldiers who approached from the parking lot. The back of his neck was red, and it definitely wasn't from the afternoon sun. It was a sure sign the situation had embarrassed him. Someone else had needed to save him, and it had happened in front of nearly a dozen soldiers. For a man who valued a strong front, that would definitely hurt.

Hannah rose and dusted grass from her uniform. She didn't offer Gabe her hand. He wouldn't take it.

Down the street, sirens wailed. Hopefully, someone was in pursuit of that truck.

Hannah drew her lips between her teeth and eyed the skid marks on the asphalt as Gabe stood beside her and straightened his gray button-down. Whoever was behind the wheel of that truck had waited for him.

This had been a targeted assault.

While the Camp McGee MPs would take point on the investigation, an attack on a recruit for Eagle Overwatch meant she would have jurisdiction as well. Given the clandestine nature of her unit, it was likely Overwatch would take over once it was proven that Gabe was the intended target.

Whether he liked it or not, their lives were interwoven for the foreseeable future.

That was a bridge she'd have to cross later. Right now, she'd interview witnesses, find out how long the truck had idled there and seek details about the driver.

Giving Gabe a second to pull himself together, Hannah spoke to the soldier closest to her. "Sergeant, find Colonel Bradenton and ask him to come out here." He'd want to be involved.

The sergeant left to obey the order, and Hannah turned back to ask Gabe what he'd seen. Only he wasn't standing next to her anymore. He was halfway across the median, headed toward his vehicle.

What was he thinking? "Gabe!" She barked his name like a command.

His posture stiffened, but he kept going as though he hadn't heard her.

She jogged to catch up to him. He couldn't leave the scene of a crime when he was the victim.

As Gabe neared the parking lot, Hannah checked for moving vehicles and then stepped off the curb in front of him, blocking his path. "Where are you going?"

"To work." He glanced down at his shirt. Grass stains smeared the right side. "Well, home to change and then to work. I've wasted an afternoon here. There's—"

"You can't leave."

His eyebrow arched high. "I can't leave? Because some dude is a terrible driver, I'm supposed to hang around?"

"Gabe, someone tried to run you down. On purpose."

"And you know this how, exactly?" He stepped to the side, and she matched his movements. "Hannah, I don't have time for this. Really. Someone wasn't watching where they were going. Wrong place, wrong time." He pinned her gaze. "We all know I'm good at that."

Surely he wasn't going to be petty about the past right now. Hannah puffed out air so hard, her bangs fluttered against her forehead. "I'm 99 percent certain you were targeted."

"Well, *ma'am*, you can't get someone arrested just because they struggled in driver's ed." He stepped around her, and his arm brushed her biceps as he passed. "Goodbye, Hannah."

She whirled and started to call after him but bit down on his name, letting it morph into a growl. She had no real cause to keep him. He pulled out of the parking lot in a midsize gray SUV, and Hannah watched until she couldn't see him any longer.

He was right. She couldn't prove this was an attack or that it was targeted.

Yet.

Nearly being mowed down in the parking lot after

walking out of a meeting with a top secret military investigative unit?

It sure didn't smell like an accident.

Huffing out her frustration, Hannah jogged past the remaining knot of onlookers and into the building.

Colonel Bradenton was waiting at the main desk. He motioned for her to follow him to the conference room and shut the door behind them. His expression said the news wasn't good.

Hannah braced herself.

The colonel shook his head, the lines on his face deeper than normal. "MPs found the vehicle three blocks from here in a housing area. Door open. Engine idling. No witnesses so far, but MPs are talking to residents."

Hannah tipped her head toward the ceiling. *Bad drivers* didn't ditch their vehicles at the first opportunity. There was a target on Gabe Buchanan's back, and someone had come straight for him.

And Hannah was the one who had put him in the crosshairs.

TWO

Kicking the door shut behind him, Gabe dropped his keys onto the half wall that separated the garage entry from the dining room. He slid his shoes off onto the hardwood and dropped his laptop over the back of the couch on his way to the kitchen.

This day could not have been any longer.

It felt like there'd been three days crammed into the twelve hours since he'd walked out of the house this morning.

Plus, he'd forgotten to eat lunch.

He walked into the kitchen and stared into the fridge. Actually, he hadn't forgotten. Knowing he was going to look Hannah in the eye again had left him too anxious to eat.

That was before a truck had nearly taken him down. Before Hannah had jumped in to save him as though he couldn't save himself.

That hadn't been embarrassing.

He grabbed a foil pan of leftover lasagna from dinner at Mona Lisa's with a small group from his church a few nights earlier and sniffed it. Still smelled okay. He pressed the bake button on the oven and threw the pan in to reheat.

He grabbed a slice of cheddar and shoved it in his mouth as he headed for the bedroom to change into sweats. He hadn't had time to change out of his grass-stained shirt earlier. An investment firm out of Des Moines was waiting on information from Skylark's profilers, which meant they were working overtime. Well, as Skylark's chief profiler and co-owner, *he* was working overtime.

His phone dinged in his hip pocket as he flipped on the bedroom light.

He'd gotten a text from an unknown number.

It's Hannah. We need to talk.

Gabe dropped the phone on his gray comforter. Nope. They didn't. He had nothing to say to the woman who had ditched him for the roommate all the girls had idolized.

Hannah hadn't been the first to succumb to Trevor's charm, but she'd been the first that Gabe had been close to. He'd been on the verge of telling her he'd fallen for her, when Trevor broke up with his girlfriend and set his sights on Hannah.

She'd totally ghosted him the minute Trevor batted his big green- or brown- or whatever-colored eyes at her.

Gabe should have asked how that had worked out for her, given Trevor's arrest, but he could never be that mean.

So, no, he wouldn't be talking to Hannah again. He didn't need another reminder that he would always come in last.

By the time he'd changed into sweatpants and a T-shirt, he'd ignored four more texts.

The three-bedroom house smelled like tomato sauce

and cheese. Pasta must be ready. He grabbed a towel, took the foil pan from the oven and then snagged a water from the fridge on his way into the den. He dropped onto the sofa and propped his feet on the coffee table.

But instead of eating, he stared at the blank screen of the television mounted on the wall over the fireplace. The pasta bowl warmed his fingers through the towel.

Hannah.

It would be awesome if he could say he hadn't thought of her in years, but that would be a lie. He thought of her too often, and now that he'd seen her again, he couldn't stop.

She'd caught his eye when she came into the coffee shop where he worked during grad school. They'd bonded over a shared love of computers.

For a little while, Gabe had thought the cute redhead was into him, and they'd started hanging out more. But she'd started coming over to the apartment, and her head had been turned pretty quickly by his roommate, Trevor Haskell. The former college basketball player had been Gabe's friend since their freshman year of undergrad, and he'd always somehow managed to make Gabe feel slightly *less than*.

And never more so than when he'd gone out with Hannah, even though he knew Gabe was interested in her.

Shortly after, Trevor was arrested for hacking into a state senator's computer and using the information he downloaded to extort money and influence votes on key legislation.

The government had moved swiftly. Trevor had broken enough laws to rack up over twenty-five years in a federal prison. Though he'd insisted he'd done nothing wrong, there had been more than enough evidence

to persuade him to enter an Alford guilty plea that de-
clared he proclaimed his innocence but realized the
case against him was strong enough for a jury to lock
him away.

Gabe had no doubt Trevor had committed those
crimes, and yet somehow, it was Gabe who'd felt guilty.
He was the one who'd run an experimental program on
Trevor's laptop and uncovered the extortion and taken
his findings to his mentor. Dr. Donovan Mathison had
insisted that Gabe call the FBI. Within months, Trevor
had been taken into custody.

Gabe rested the cooling lasagna on his stomach. Dr.
Mathison had died less than a year ago, and no one else
knew it was Gabe who had made that call. Not even
Hannah, who had disappeared within days of Trevor's
arrest.

Seeing her today... It had been a long time since he'd
felt this low. This second-best. This guilty.

He forked a piece of lukewarm lasagna into his mouth
and chewed. His jaw protested the movement. While he
wasn't too sore from smashing into the ground, his chin
had caught it pretty good when his head hit the grass.

There had been no need for her to take him down
that way. He'd have moved before the truck hit him.

Maybe.

He'd heard the engine but hadn't turned fast enough.
If she hadn't tackled him, he might be a smear on the
pavement at Camp McGee right now.

Was somebody after him because he'd talked to Hannah about her supersecret spy group?

With a snort, he shoved in another bite of lasagna.
Nobody even knew he'd been to Camp McGee for that
meeting except for the three of them who had been

in that room. Not even his business partner. He'd told Leigh he had an appointment, but nothing more.

His phone dinged on the coffee table yet again.

Enough was enough.

Setting his dinner next to his tablet, he snatched up the phone, prepared to give Hannah a piece of his mind, to let loose with all of the things he'd thought about her over the years, whether they were kind or true or not.

I'm serious. We need to talk. I'm sitting outside.

This was some serious stalker-level behavior. She hadn't seemed the type back in the day.

Then again, she hadn't seemed the type to turn her back on him for his roommate either.

Gabe dialed the phone before he could change his mind. As soon as she answered, he started in on his tirade. She didn't get to talk first. "What are you thinking? I said no to the job. Keep your spy stuff to yourself. I don't want it. And I'm really not interested in resuming any kind of friendship. That ship sailed, Hannah. A long time ago." *But given that Trevor has no internet access in prison, I'm sure he'd love a handwritten letter from his last girlfriend.*

Saying that would just reveal that he was still hurt over the way she'd treated him.

"I heard you today. Loud and clear. That's not why I'm calling." Her voice was brusque, though it held a thread of urgency.

Gabe said nothing. He ought to hang up, but the same curiosity that had driven him to attend the meeting today kept the phone pressed to his ear now.

"I'm calling about the truck that tried to run you down."

"Like I said, wrong place, wrong time. Someone can't drive, that's—"

"The truck was stolen."

"Okay. All the more reason for the driver to make a fast getaway."

She sighed. The sound was a rough scrape against his ear. "The truck was stolen from a gas station less than a mile from the post. It was found abandoned within minutes of the incident."

"Meaning?"

"Meaning the intent was to harm you. No more. No less."

This was out of control. He was a cyberpsychologist who spent his days profiling job candidates. "Hannah, nobody wants me dead."

"Someone stole a truck, drove it directly to your location, waited for you to walk out of a building and gunned straight for you."

Gabe shook his head. She was wrong. Maybe they'd been after her or someone else in her unit. He wasn't the target. "You said you're in front of my house?"

"In the driveway."

"Leave."

He hung up the phone and tossed it onto the couch beside him. This day had brought up enough memories to keep him awake for the rest of the night. The last thing he needed was to add a false narrative about his life being in danger. That would be—

There was a distant click, and the house went dark.

What just happened?

Hannah's head jerked up from her phone, and she stared at the front of Gabe's A-frame home. It was nestled among the trees in the mountains between Flat

Rock and Brevard. Something was different about it though.

While the rest of the houses half-hidden in the trees on the narrow gravel road were lit, Gabe's had gone dark. The lights on the deck and over the garage had been burning seconds earlier. Now they were out.

Either Gabe had managed to shut everything down at once, or someone had cut the power.

Gabe had told her to leave, but there was no way she could. Not now. She texted him with one hand as she reached for the door with the other. *You okay?*

Three dots.

Nothing.

Three dots.

Yes.

She bumped the car door shut with her hip.

Stay where you are. I'm checking outside.

No response.

Drawing her SIG, she stepped carefully toward the house, listening. There was only the normal noises of the mountains at night, nothing that seemed out of place. Circling to the backyard, she scanned what she could see of a sloped, grassy area that ended at a tree line. The yard near the house was flat and boasted a small patio that held a couple of wooden chaises and a charcoal grill. A split-rail fence ran along both sides of the yard, but the neighbors' houses weren't visible through the trees.

Peeking around the corner, Hannah surveyed the side of the A-frame. Still no sign of life, not even near the electrical box where the power lines entered the house. Flicking on her flashlight, she checked the box and the damp ground beneath. There were no signs of tampering. No footprints or broken grass marred the area. Yet there was no power.

Making her way to the front, she scanned the power line from the siding to the pole on the street. It seemed to be intact. Finally, she mounted the front deck stairs, holstered her sidearm and knocked.

Gabe answered. He held the phone to his ear and glared at her through the glass storm door as though this was somehow her fault.

It might be, given that she'd been the one to float his name to Overwatch. Clearly, someone didn't want him anywhere near the top secret unit or her fledgling team.

She swallowed the self-recrimination. There'd be plenty of time later to worry about whether Gabe was in danger because of her. She was probably going to lie awake watching the clock tick off the minutes until dawn. But right now, she needed to find out why Gabe's house was dark.

"Can I come in?"

His expression didn't change, but he unlocked the storm door, shoved it open and stepped aside as she entered. She locked both doors behind her and tipped her head toward his phone. "Power company?"

He offered a curt nod.

"Where's your electrical panel?" She doubted anyone was in the house, but she needed to be sure.

"In the hall. I checked. It's fine."

Hannah dug her teeth into her lower lip. She'd told him to stay put, not to wander the dark house where who knew what could be lurking.

While he navigated the company's customer service

menu, Hannah made her way up the hallway by flashlight. The refinished hardwood creaked with each step.

At any other time, that sound would be comforting, a reminder of the many times she and her siblings had spent the night at their grandparents' home as children. Her grandmother would step lightly up the hallway to peek in on her sleeping grandchildren, her approach betrayed by the old floorboards.

That had been before their mother had abandoned them and Hannah's world had been turned upside down.

Shaking her shoulders to shed the memories, Hannah opened the electrical panel and scanned the switches. None had been tripped. Slamming the metal door shut with a clang, she listened to Gabe give his name and address. He must have reached a human. His voice took on a hard edge as he repeated his name slowly and then spelled it.

When she walked into the den, she pinned him in the beam from her flashlight. He winced and turned away, still speaking into the phone, this time spelling his street name. During the long pause as he listened, his eyebrows knit together. "That's impossible. Can I speak to a supervisor?" Barely sheathed frustration edged his words.

It was likely the customer service agent had no idea that annoyance was there, but it was a familiar tone she recognized. He'd perfected it in grad school when he had to deal with difficult customers at the coffee shop. Civility layered over annoyance. It was too sweet to be real.

Hannah clamped down on a smile. That long-ago Gabe had been fun. A good friend. Attractive without knowing he was attractive.

Too bad their entire friendship had been a lie.

She rubbed her fingers over her mouth to wipe away the amusement. One day soon, he'd find out that she'd used him. Would the truth make him angrier? Or would he understand and forgive?

"Thank you." With a loud exhale, Gabe let the phone fall onto the couch and then dropped beside it. He laid his head on the back cushion and dragged his hands down his face.

Hannah arched an eyebrow. "Light bill wasn't paid?" Seemed like an awfully big coincidence given the circumstances.

With a hefty sigh, Gabe lifted his head only slightly to look at her and then dropped it again. "Apparently, I don't exist."

"Meaning?"

"Meaning my name, my address, my account number... None of them exist in the power company's database."

Hannah sank to the edge of an armless chair by the fireplace. "Somebody wiped you off their computer?"

"It's a glitch." Bracing his hands on the couch beside his thighs, he slid back and sat up to study her. "I was in their computers two days ago when the automatic payment went out to cover my bill."

Could he not see what was going on here? The Gabe she remembered was ridiculously intelligent. Fluent in reading people. It was what made him so good at his job. His brain was able to marry personality and online behavior into a deep, workable profile. He could not only analyze past behavior but could anticipate next steps that even the people he was profiling didn't see coming.

Right now, denial was working on his head. There was no way he wasn't seeing this. She eased closer to the edge of the chair, letting her flashlight dangle between her knees. The light cast dancing shadows around the room. "Do you not get that all of this is connected?"

He looked her dead in the eye for the first time. Shadows made his face seem menacing, less like Gabe and more like some of the criminals she'd taken down over the years.

Including Trevor.

"All of what is connected?" His voice was low. This time, he wasn't hiding his frustration behind false courtesy. "You want to put a truck thief and my lights going out together? That's a stretch." He stood, walked to the front door and pulled it open. Unlocking the storm door, he gestured toward the street. "I've had a long day."

Hannah stood, killed the flashlight and pocketed the device. She could argue, but he'd just lock his attitude tighter and plug his ears more. Although Camp McGee was less than an hour away, she'd book a hotel tonight so she'd be available if something else happened to Gabe.

Truthfully, she'd probably end up spending the night parked on the road a few houses away to make sure Gabe was safe if someone made another run at him.

He'd call it stalking.

She called it playing things safe.

She pulled a business card from her hip pocket and laid it on the mantel. "My number. If anything happens, call me."

"Nothing is going to happen."

Hannah walked across the room and stopped in front of where Gabe stood like a doorman, waiting for her to exit.

Aside from her earlier tackle, this was the closest she'd been to him in years. Only inches apart, she looked at him head-on. She was very aware that he'd filled out since grad school. His chest was broader, and he had a more confident stance.

But something in his face told her that his confidence was nothing more than a front.

She studied him in the dim light, but his expression never changed. "You're so resistant to everything I have to say. Why did you bother to show up for that meeting today?"

Something flickered in his gaze. It looked like hurt. Maybe sadness. Tough to say in the near darkness.

He tipped his chin so they were eye to eye, only inches apart. "I don't know." The words were low. Honest.

It was the most real emotion he'd shown her since the day he'd asked why she'd chosen Trevor over him.

She'd been unable to answer.

Hannah merely nodded. Their past needed to stay in the past, but the present charged forward, demanding attention. She stepped out the door and listened to him lock the deadbolt behind her.

Whether Gabe liked it or not, she was keeping watch on the house. Tonight, she'd call Dana Santiago and have her start investigating the attack on his account at the power company. Overwatch's tech consultant was the best out there and would likely have the hacker's name by morning.

Hannah hoped so. Because while they shared a past Gabe might never understand, Hannah needed to make sure that involving Gabe in Overwatch didn't destroy his future.

THREE

Gabe pulled one arm across his chest, trying to stretch the tension from his upper back as he studied the monitors on his standing desk. The light in his office at Skylark was dimmed to ease his nagging headache, sinking the pale gray walls into shadows and intensifying the glare that spilled in from windows that faced the hall.

Four monitors sat in an arc in front of him, following the curve of the desktop. Two displayed the work history and an online profile of a candidate for the investment firm in Des Moines. A third held the beginnings of Gabe's report on the woman. The fourth was open to his Hype Connect profile, which he'd long ago set to private.

That screen held his attention. As he stretched his other arm, he stared at the three faces smiling out at him from the deep, dark yesterday of social media. In that particular moment, after a shift behind the counter at Bean and Gone, he wore a black apron smeared with whipped cream.

He'd never understood whipped cream on coffee.

His arm was slung casually across Hannah's shoulders. She looked so young. She was dressed in black leggings and an oversize Brevard College sweatshirt.

Her red hair had been past her shoulders then, and it was piled on top of her head in one of those twisty things girls did. Behind them, Trevor was a bug-eyed, wide-mouthed photo bomber.

He tried to study the picture from an unbiased perspective. From the outside, it looked as though he and Hannah were close. A "thing." It also appeared that Trevor was the goof who'd been shoved into the friend zone.

It had almost been that way. In fact, the day that photo was taken, Gabe had been a breath away from asking Hannah to step out of that zone with him and go on a real date. She'd pretty much stolen his heart over the months they'd hung out together.

Literally a minute after that photo was snapped by another barista, Trevor had announced he'd broken up with his latest girlfriend. All it had taken was four seconds of Trevor's flirting for Hannah to completely forget Gabe's name.

He couldn't believe she was that much of a flake, that she would fall for the frat-boy party image Trevor tossed around as easily as he tossed women aside.

Shortly after, when Trevor had been arrested, Hannah had vanished. Phone calls had gone straight to voice mail. Texts had gone unanswered. DMs unread.

Until the very last day he worked at Bean and Gone, he'd watched the door, certain she'd return.

She hadn't.

He let his gaze slip to his own image, although he hated photos of himself. Back then, he was trying to figure out who he was. The taunts of the kids from elementary through high school had grown silent in college, but the echoes had still reverberated in his soul. He was a computer geek before it was cool. The kid with all of the wrong clothes, wrong hair, wrong everything.

The "cool" kids had never let him forget it. Although the bruises had faded, the memory of the taunts never had.

Sure, he was an adult now, and he recognized that he was more than his outward appearance, that others didn't get to judge what he wore or how he spent his free time. That didn't mean the scars weren't still tender.

He cringed at the grad school version of himself, back when he'd worn his dark hair to his shoulders because everyone else did. When he'd gone to the gym religiously because everyone else did. When he'd joined the superhero craze and had worn all of the T-shirts because everyone else did.

He didn't even like those movies, although he could tell you the backstory of every Marvel character that had ever graced the screen.

Because everyone else knew.

None of that had gotten him the girl who supposedly loved both superheroes and long-haired guys who were semifit. Nope. Hannah had gone for the tall, skinny, blond basketball player who watched sports and shoot-'em-up action movies.

Story of his life.

"Gabe, you got that profile ready yet?"

He jumped as a voice from the present shattered the memories of the past. When he looked up, Leigh Lewis, co-owner of Skylark Profiling, stood in the doorway.

Gabe slid his wireless mouse to the side and minimized the photo.

Leigh studied him with one blond eyebrow arched, the corner of her mouth following its lead into a half smile. "What are you doing that makes you so jumpy?"

He definitely wasn't about to confess that he was tripping down memory lane. "Engrossed in the job and sleep-deprived from trying to make the electric company recognize that my house and I really do exist."

She winced. "How's that going?"

Gabe had spent his drive in to the office on the phone with a supervisor at the utility, the supervisor's supervisor, and finally, their boss. "Someone is doing a drive-by today for a physical look at the house and to check the meter. I sent a ton of paperwork in to them as soon as I walked in the door. We'll go from there."

"Maybe they'll reset you to zero and you won't have to pay the bill this month."

"Funny, but no. I paid it a couple of days ago."

"No joy there, then." Leigh stepped into the room and walked around the desk to look at his screen. "Any red flags on this woman? Assurance Trust Financial thinks she's their new CFO."

"Nothing yet." Then again, he'd spent the past fifteen minutes not focused on the job, so he was a little behind. "Give me a half hour, and I'll have the full report ready."

He'd met Leigh during his last semester in grad school, and they'd discovered they worked well together. Leigh and her husband led the financial side of the business, while Gabe headed up the actual profiling. The arrangement freed him to work the way he wanted without having to worry about logistics.

"Maybe this would go faster if you'd run it through that genius program you created in grad school." Leigh's voice went from teasing to serious so fast Gabe's head nearly spun in a circle.

Not that he needed conversational whiplash. Her statement rocked his foundation. "What?" No one knew about that program, outside his grad school mentor, who'd passed away the previous year.

"It's a rumor I just heard."

"Well, there is no program." Forcing himself to turn away from her, Gabe scanned the screen. The candidate had a basic social media presence. No red flags. Just vacation photos and pics of her grandkids. "You know better than to listen to gossip, especially in the tech world." Still, who would be talking about a program he'd buried nearly a decade ago?

Leigh shrugged. "Rumors often have a kernel of truth."

He tensed. This one did, but it was old history he would never discuss, not since that program had led to Trevor's undoing. "Like I said, if you'll give me about half an hour to—"

"Gabe, we need to talk."

This voice from the doorway jolted through him in a different way. What was Hannah doing here? He'd made it clear that he wanted nothing to do with her or that job offer, hadn't he?

At least her presence made Leigh back down.

Hannah strode into the room, wearing a visitor's pass. She was all authority, as though his office belonged to her and *he* was the interloper.

It ought to tick him off, but something about Leigh's posture beside him stopped the anger from bubbling up.

His partner was on high alert, tensing at the intrusion. She stepped around his desk and blocked Hannah's view of Gabe.

Since when was she so protective?

"Can I help you? I'm Leigh Lewis, cofounder of Skylark Profiling."

It was Gabe's turn to raise an eyebrow. Cofounder?

She didn't throw that around often. First the rumors about that old program and now the mama-bear routine. What had she eaten for breakfast this morning? Her usual egg white and turkey bacon on wheat didn't produce this kind of behavior.

There was a long pause. While he'd had little experience with Hannah as an investigator, he knew from the way she'd charged into his house last night that she wasn't going to back down easily.

Gabe leaned slightly to the side, catching a glimpse of her over Leigh's shoulder.

She didn't look his way. Instead, she reached into the pocket of the gray blazer she wore over a dark blue button-down and jeans. She produced what looked like a wallet and held it up inches from Leigh's nose. "Chief Warrant Officer Hannah Austin. US Army special investigations."

Leigh wasn't one to back down easily herself, but after only a slight hesitation, she nodded. "How can I help you?"

Pocketing her credentials, Hannah glanced around the room, carefully avoiding Gabe's gaze. "I need to speak to Gabriel Buchanan. It's about an investigation that doesn't concern your company, but thank you for the offer to help. I'll let you know if I need anything."

Leigh drummed her manicured fingernails against her jean-clad thigh. He'd never figured out how she managed to type with those talons.

"Fine." She turned to Gabe, flipping her blond hair over her shoulder. "If anything proprietary about the company is involved, I want to be present."

With a scathing look that raked Hannah from head to toe, Leigh stepped around her and headed out the door, boot heels thunking on the dark industrial carpet.

That. Was. Weird.

Now he was left to deal with Hannah. Again.

Gabe shoved his hands into his pockets and balled his fists, trying to reconcile her presence to his reality. Just a couple of minutes before, he'd been looking at an old picture of her, the girl he'd hard-core crushed on to the point of sleeplessness. Now she stood in front of him, that demanding look he was beginning to dislike creasing her forehead with deep lines.

Everything about this situation irritated him. "I told you last night we have nothing more to say to each other."

"Did you?" Without waiting for an answer, she shut his office door and walked over to stand directly across the desk from him. "You have bigger problems than you think you do."

Yeah, he did. And every single one of them was standing in front of him wrapped up in blue jeans and a blazer. "I had zero problems until I showed up at your meeting yesterday."

She actually flinched so hard that he almost felt bad about speaking, although he had no idea why his words had drawn that kind of response.

Just as quickly as her control had slipped, Hannah reset it. "We ran a background check on you."

They couldn't do that. He should know. His career was based on that kind of thing. "You need my permission to—"

"Not for this job."

What in the world had she gotten him into? And what was wrong with his background check? He was clean. "I've got nothing to hide."

"No, you don't. When we pulled it last week, you were spotless. Just one speeding ticket to mar the perfection. If I didn't know you, I'd say you were in WITSEC, your record is so polished." Her expression tightened, and worry coated her features, overriding the professionalism she was clearly trying to hide behind.

"So what's the problem?" The sooner she told him, the sooner she'd leave. The sooner he could start pretending he wasn't still drawn to her.

"In light of what happened with the power company, I asked my people to run it again, just to see if something weird was going on."

"Okay?"

"Gabriel Anthony Buchanan?" She braced her hands on the desk and leaned toward him. "You no longer exist."

Gabe dragged his hands down his cheeks and looked to the ceiling. "I'm starting to think there's something very wrong with you."

He didn't know how close he was to the truth. Or how far. While Hannah had no idea what was happening, it was clear that reaching out to Gabe had set off a firestorm. "I'm not making this up. Run a background check on yourself."

With a heavy sigh, he complied.

He probably didn't want to humor what he clearly believed was an insane delusion, but he also likely figured the quickest way to get her to leave was to prove her wrong.

How she wished he could.

She sincerely hoped he would.

Gabe clicked the mouse and paused. His brow furrowed. He clicked again. Typed.

Glancing at her, he turned to the far-right screen, adjusted the monitor toward him and frowned deeper.

Suddenly, he was all motion. He walked around the desk, jogged to the door and yanked it open, leaving her to trail him as he rushed up the hallway. He walked into an office without knocking, and Hannah followed, waiting in the doorway.

The statuesque blonde, Leigh Lewis, stood at a tall desk much like Gabe's.

Did none of these people know what a chair was?

Leigh's head snapped up as Gabe walked to her desk. "Pull up my files."

Her gaze flickered from Gabe to Hannah and back. "The ones you're working on? They should be in—"

"My account log-ins. My employee records. A background check. Anything."

Leigh lifted both hands from the keyboard and stepped away from her desk. "If the government wants something that's in our system, they need a warrant."

Waving a dismissive hand at Hannah, Gabe leaned closer to Leigh. "For my eyes only. Show me that my information is there."

It looked like Leigh wasn't going to comply.

If she wanted a warrant, Hannah could have one here faster than the blonde woman who had been standing uncomfortably close to Gabe only a few moments earlier could ever imagine.

Before Hannah could reach for her phone, Leigh waved Gabe around the desk and started typing.

Like Gabe before her, she stopped and stared. She typed more.

Behind her, Gabe dragged his hand across his mouth. "I'm not there."

"I don't…" Leigh picked up her phone and started texting. "I'm getting Quentin Fisher on this. You're not in payroll. None of your employee evals are here. Your log-ins are here, but the rest is…gone. It's like you—"

"Don't exist." Gabe sagged against the wall, eyes fixed on Leigh's central computer monitor.

Dropping her phone to the desk, Leigh rounded the corner and advanced on Hannah. She stopped inches away. "What have you done?"

Hannah tried not to wince. There was no doubt the assaults on Gabe's life and identity had been launched because Hannah had offered him a position with Overwatch. This was on her head, but this Leigh woman didn't have to know that.

She stood her ground as Leigh attempted to tower over her, even though the other woman was about an inch shorter, even in heeled boots. Hannah had faced down her share of bullies, and Leigh had the potential to become one quickly, thanks to her anger and confusion.

"I didn't do a thing," Hannah said evenly. "My job is to protect Gabe, to figure out who is behind this and to put a stop to it."

Leigh's icy, blue eyes scanned hers, searching for something, before she backed down and walked to her desk to resume her position.

Gabe hadn't moved. He still stood as though events were catching up to him so fast that they were draining his strength. "You should have let that truck hit me. It would have been easier than this."

"Wait." Leigh whirled on him. "What truck?"

"Not now, Leigh. I'm a lot more concerned with figuring out why my identity has been wiped. I tried to run a background check on myself before we came in here, but I came up empty."

"Let me try." She started to click her mouse, then stopped and looked directly at Gabe. "Does this have anything to do with the meeting you went to on Camp McGee yesterday?"

Interesting. Gabe had mentioned offhand the day before that his business partner had no idea he was attending a sit-down about another job, so how had Leigh found out?

Hannah wanted to dive into full investigative mode, but she held back. More information would pour out of these two if she simply made herself invisible.

Leigh avoided looking at Gabe, staring instead at the screen before her.

"How did you know where I was?" he asked.

"You carried your work phone with you. When you were late getting back, I pinged it to make sure you hadn't driven off the side of a mountain."

Leigh Lewis tracked movements through work-issued devices? Seemed like an invasion of privacy, unless the function could be turned off at will on the user end. It was hard to imagine someone would agree to—

"Cell phones." Gabe's exclamation rang through the room. He reached into his pocket and pulled out a phone in a red-and-gray case. MIT colors. His genius undergrad alma mater. He'd moved to Asheville to customize his doctorate at the smaller Blue Ridge University outside the town.

Punching the screen with his thumb, Gabe shook his head, his expression dark. "No service."

No service meant he had no account. Someone was wiping him out of every database they could find. It was a creeping virus of destruction. If this didn't end soon, every piece of his identity that was accessible online would be destroyed. He'd be unable to function in a digital world.

Someone with a long reach was behind this if they could hack that many databases.

Stepping into the hallway, Hannah dialed a number on her cell.

Dana Santiago answered on the first ring. "What's up, Hannah Banana?"

Seriously, that needed to stop. It was so…ancient. And a little silly. But that was how Overwatch's head of technology rolled since she'd become a mother to an adorable little girl.

"I need you to drop what you're doing and get on something quick." She detailed what was happening to Gabe.

Dana was clicking away at her keyboard before the story ended. "Do you want me to see what scraps of his identity I can rescue? Or do you want me to try to trace it? If I can catch a breach as it's happening, I might be able to track where it's coming from."

"Stop them from wiping him out. Start with bank accounts, brokerage accounts, things like that."

The tapping stopped. "You realize those are probably the first things they hit, right?"

"It's worth a shot. Keep me updated."

"On it." The call ended.

Gabe blew out the door, heading up the hall toward his office at top speed.

By the time Hannah caught up, he was behind his desk. She didn't wait to be invited and walked around it to stare over his shoulder.

He was pulling up the Hype Connect social media platform.

Gabe still had a profile? Hannah had asked Dana to help scrub her social media presence long ago, partially due to the nature of her job and partially due to the increasing nastiness that social media spewed.

Gabe's log-in failed. He tried twice more. It failed both times.

Tension radiated off him. He held up a hand as though he was going to speak, then he balled his fist and rested it on the desk beside the keyboard, almost as though he was trying to keep everything inside of him from bursting forth. "I was logged in when you showed up."

"So whoever is worming their way around the world, scrubbing you out of existence, is working right now?" Hannah texted that detail to Dana. Maybe they could catch up to the hacker at the Hype Connect site. "Any other social media?"

"No." He faced her, though they stood only inches apart. "And that one was private. I only kept it because it's the only record I have of college. My parents' house burned down a few years ago. I kept saying I was going to download the photos, but now they're…gone."

If the account was private and hadn't been updated since college, how had someone located it? And why had he been logged on when she walked into the room?

College. The time in his life when she'd slipped in, befriended him in order to get closer to Trevor Haskell and then disappeared after Trevor's arrest.

Her first undercover mission. Trevor had been suspicious that someone might be after him, so it had made sense to move slowly. To come at him through a friend.

A fact Gabe still didn't know.

At some point though, Gabe had become more than a means to an end. He'd become a friend. Something more could've come of things if they had been regular students. If she'd really been studying criminal justice at Brevard College and not trying to bring down a hacker who was attempting to influence public policy.

Her attraction to Gabe was the reason she'd cut ties and walked away as soon as Trevor was in custody. Her career was too new. She couldn't be marked forever as the "girl" who fell for an asset on her first assignment.

Somewhere in Gabe's social media profile, there were memories about her. He'd been looking at them this morning, remembering.

Hannah hated herself. She was responsible for his pain in the past. She was responsible for his pain now. The truth sliced into her chest and left her bleeding.

Gabe sank against the desk, bracing his hands on either side of his hips. "What do I do?"

"You let Chief Warrant Officer Austin protect you." Leigh stood at the door, arms crossed. "Go home, Gabe. Let her handle this. Whatever is going on, it's not going to get fixed while you're here." When Gabe started to protest, she held up her hand and stepped into the room. "You and I both know you can't be here right now. We can't risk Skylark when someone is hacking in to delete everything you're working on. Quentin is tightening the firewall and locking down access as we speak to stop any further intrusions." She inhaled slowly. "But he says your work files have been completely wiped."

"No." Gabe dove for his computer and started typing. "Everything I was working on for Des Moines—"

"Is destroyed."

FOUR

Slowing at an intersection on the drive to his house, Gabe glanced in the rearview, where Hannah followed in an inconspicuous midsize blue SUV. She'd wanted him to ride with her, but he resented the implication that he couldn't take care of himself on the fifteen-minute drive home and, frankly, he'd needed to process the past twenty-four hours.

Instead of being therapeutic, the silence gave his brain too much time to spin theoreticals. He needed a sounding board, someone to help him talk through the mud. He had his work phone, which hadn't been hit by whatever was eating his identity, so there was no reason he couldn't reach out, but to whom?

He couldn't call his parents. They tended to worry anytime he was stressed, scarred by the fallout from their son's struggles at the hands of bullies in his younger years. He had no siblings. Friends wouldn't grasp the enormity of the situation.

He tapped the steering wheel. "Call Jeanette Mathison."

Hopefully, she wasn't in a meeting. The widow of his grad school mentor was a corporate lawyer in Asheville. She'd be a caring yet unbiased ear.

"Gabe. Are you calling because you have time for lunch?" Mrs. Mathison answered on the first ring with her standard greeting. Based on the sounds around her, she was working. He could almost see her tapping away at her laptop. She was in her late sixties, gray-haired and trim, and she was always in motion. Always happy to hear from him. And, like a mother, she was always hoping for a visit.

"Sadly, no. Do you have a minute?"

"What's wrong?"

"How do you know something's wrong?"

"Because I know your voice as well as I used to know my own son's. He could never hide when he was in trouble, and you're using that same tone right now." Her son, Hunter Mathison, was a true prodigal. Drugs and alcohol had driven him from his parents before Gabe met them. He'd briefly returned for his father's funeral the previous year before vanishing again.

Gabe's heart ached for Jeanette. Maybe he shouldn't dump his problems on her, but he'd already started the conversation, and she'd worry if he didn't elaborate. "Just some weirdness." He laid out the events of the morning. "I'm trying to wrap my head around the ram-ifications."

"Gabe." She exhaled loudly. "The ramifications are huge. No social, no driver's license, no bank accounts? No email or phone? I can't imagine what would hap-pen if you were pulled over for speeding. You'd likely be brought in by federal authorities and treated like a terrorist."

"Great."

"You can stay at the house while the authorities fig-ure this out. I do have electricity, you know."

It was tempting. The Mathisons had always treated

him like family, particularly when he was working on his doctorate with Dr. Donovan Mathison.

But after Trevor had been arrested, he'd set aside the program he'd developed and hadn't touched it since. There was only one copy left, and he'd tucked it away on an encrypted external drive where no one would find it.

He slowed to turn onto his street. "I'm almost home. Just…pray for me." Not so long ago, he wouldn't have made such a request. Now it was a natural first step.

Although his nemesis was hiding in the darkness, God could still see them.

"Keep me posted. And if you need a safe place to land…"

"I know. Thanks. Take care." He disconnected the call as he punched the garage door opener and then pulled inside.

Hannah parked behind him and walked into the garage as he exited his SUV, shadowing him as he entered the house. She was hovering, watching… Way too close. He didn't need her here. Didn't want her here.

But he'd already learned there was no use arguing. Her investigative unit had decided he was a commodity that needed to be protected, whether he liked it or not.

Gabe dropped his keys on the ledge by the door and was three steps into the room before he realized the lights were on. "How did that happen?"

Sliding her low black boots onto the hardwood next to his, Hannah followed him into the space between the living room and the dining room. "I pulled some strings."

"What strings?"

"When you work for the federal government, there are lots of strings. Sometimes they tie you up, but other times…" She shrugged as though this was no big thing.

"What exactly is it that you do for the government?" The little sales pitch he'd attended yesterday had been vague at best. There had been talk of the investigations and of undercover operations, but nothing concrete.

Since he wasn't interested, he'd only half listened. He'd been too distracted by seeing Hannah again and had also been following a chart in his head of the Des Moines candidate's behavior both online and off-line.

That work was at a standstill now. Fortunately, he'd backed his files up to his hard drive, and Quentin didn't think that had been compromised. Still, it wasn't like Gabe could wrap up what he'd started, not when he'd been banned from touching his work until someone gave him his life back.

He could no longer deny that there was something going on. Something that involved Hannah and the job she was oddly silent about.

Gabe stepped to the side, blocking her way farther into his home. "What's the job, Hannah?"

She looked at him directly, drawing his attention away from his circumstances and fully to her. He'd managed to forget that her eyes were the deepest, clearest green he'd ever seen.

He cleared his throat and shifted his gaze over her shoulder. While she wasn't an enemy, she certainly wasn't his friend.

She lifted an eyebrow. "I'm a team leader in a military investigative service."

"NCIS? OSI?" He knew them all. In his line of work, he'd built candidate profiles for many companies that hired former military.

"Given that I'm in the Army and not in the Navy or the Air Force…"

"You're not with CID though." Yesterday, the colonel had made it clear that the job opportunity before him wasn't with the US Army Criminal Investigation Division.

She shook her head. "I can only read you in so far."

"CIA?" That was some deep stuff that he didn't want to touch.

"CIA?" Hannah chuckled, dragging her hand through the top of her hair. "No."

It was almost as though she delighted in frustrating him, like there was a game in progress and only she knew the rules. "Can we stop being cryptic?"

"Can we sit down?"

Gabe flung his hand toward the living room and then followed as she took a seat in the chair she'd briefly occupied the night before.

He sank to the edge of his sofa, wishing he could put on sweats, binge-watch '90s sitcoms, and down a frozen pizza. Anything, really, other than sit through this tense situation he was in.

It was like living in a nightmare.

Hannah cleared her throat. "You weren't paying attention yesterday, were you?"

Busted. "Let's pretend I wasn't."

With an amused smirk, she crossed her ankles and tucked them beneath the chair, her posture so straight she looked like a queen. That was nowhere close to the way she used to sit cross-legged, literally everywhere she landed. "My team is involved in investigations at high levels. We tend to get called in when the corruption runs deep or when it's not clear where the action is. My unit acts independently of any other unit. It's… complicated."

"People usually say that about relationships." Okay, he shouldn't have said that, given his past feelings. He switched gears before she could follow him down that road. "So, why me?"

Steepling her fingers, she pressed the tips to her lips and studied him as though he held the answer to his own question. "I've been with the unit for several years, and I've been assigned a new team that will operate out of northern Georgia and eastern Tennessee."

"That's not an area with a hefty military population."

"It's a base of operations." For the first time, she looked uncertain. "While I can't give you specifics, I can tell you that our teams consist of investigative personnel as well as support personnel. What I need is someone who can rip into a hard drive from a distance or who can access—"

"I don't hack." Not anymore. He'd toyed with it in undergrad until he'd started to chase the high that came with it. It wasn't a path he wanted to follow.

"But I know you could. White-hat hackers are big in my field. And you're special." She actually flushed and sank her teeth into her lower lip. "What I mean is, you're cross-skilled. You know tech and you can pro-file as well. I can use someone like you."

"Why not?" Gabe rose and looked down at her from across the room, the terminology she'd employed rak-ing his nerves. "You've used me in the past. Might as well keep up the trend."

Ouch. Too much. He'd let her see the scar she'd left behind. The one he'd have preferred to hide forever.

"You don't understand—" She stood suddenly, slic-ing the air with her hand. "Never mind. I'm sorry. For all of that. And I'm sorry for what's happening to you today."

"Today? How is today your fault?"

"I'm pretty sure that interviewing you put you on

somebody's radar. And they may want to go past ruining your life." She planted her hands on her hips. "It's possible they want you dead."

Hannah sat on an old recliner in the guest room with her feet propped on the bed. Gabe had never fully agreed to her staying in the house to protect him, but he'd never kicked her out either.

Small victories.

They'd spent an awkward afternoon on a conference call to headquarters with Dana, trying to piece together the broken pieces of Gabe's life. In her opinion, things might not be as dire as they'd initially seemed. Gabe still existed, though things had been buried or encrypted in ways Hannah didn't fully understand and that Dana was still puzzling out.

Now, with a pizza on the way for dinner, Gabe had disappeared into his basement gym while Hannah took a few minutes of quiet to breathe.

In the decade since she'd last seen Gabe, she'd thought of him more often than she should. Back then, on her first assignment, she hadn't fully developed the thick skin necessary to be ruthless. And given that she'd used Gabe to get to Trevor…

She'd seen the look on his face today when she'd thoughtlessly said the word *use* in reference to needing him on her fledgling team. He thought she'd used him in the past because she had a crush on his roommate. If only she could tell him the truth, that she'd been investigating Trevor…

That she'd made the rookie mistake of falling for Gabe.

But given that Trevor had filed appeal after appeal, it wasn't safe to let Gabe know he'd been an asset during her undercover investigation, no matter how much she wanted to tell him.

Even vetting him for her team had proven to be dangerous.

So far, no one had been able to find any hint of who would want Gabe to stay away from her new team. Not everyone bought that some adversary wanted him dead. Even Dana had asked why they'd go to the trouble of wiping him from the system if the plan was to kill him.

But Hannah couldn't forget that this had started with a physical attack. When that hadn't proved successful, the enemy had tried a different tactic. Erasing Gabe's life was a malicious act that spoke to a special, personal sort of hatred. One that said they weren't afraid to toy with him.

Somebody was taking great pleasure in watching him suffer.

But who?

The likeliest suspect was Trevor Haskell, but he had no idea it was Gabe who had turned him in to the FBI. He also had no access to technology. The limited amount he was allowed to use in prison was under heavy supervision. The sorts of hacks required to wipe Gabe out of the system would take more time, resources and freedom than Trevor had.

Hannah rubbed her temple, fighting a growing headache. It had been a long time since she'd faced down a migraine. Now definitely wasn't the time to work one up. Her body and brain needed to be fully engaged if she was going to figure out who was assaulting Gabe.

Leigh Lewis was a possibility, but there was no potential motive, just means. A tech geek like Leigh easily had the time and resources to shred Gabe's identity.

Skylark Profiling also had access to an untold number of databases due to their online profiling. They'd even done some work for the government, which gave them even more open doors. Still, it was one thing to access a database. It was another thing entirely to wipe a person out of it. Gabe had been hit on every imaginable front, from identifiers as big as his social security number to as trivial as private social media accounts.

That was the work of a seriously powerful hacker.

She'd have Dana start digging into every known—

Her phone rang the three short trills that indicated her sister was calling. The sound thrummed against her rapidly intensifying headache. As soon as this phone call with Zoe was done, she was asking Gabe if he had any pain relievers.

Zoe was a junior at Brevard College, majoring in criminal justice. It didn't exactly thrill Hannah that Zoe was following in her footsteps. Hopefully she'd take a less dangerous, behind-the-scenes investigative role and not one that put her in the line of fire.

Hannah would never forgive herself if something happened to her sister, or to her brother Eli, who'd given her a ton of stress by joining the military two years before.

She pressed the screen and lifted the phone to her ear. "Is everything okay?" Zoe rarely called, preferring to text or communicate through social media messages instead.

"You always answer that way, and everything is always okay. I'm an adult. You can lay down the big-sister mantle you've been wearing since we were kids."

Hannah sat straight up. "Somebody's full of sass today." Zoe was typically one of those quick-to-listen-and-slow-to-speak people. She was the sibling who looked before she leaped, then measured the distance just to be sure she'd jumped properly.

"Sorry." Zoe puffed out a breath. "Are you busy?"

The room seemed to tilt sideways, and Hannah's stomach swayed in a sickening dip.

She massaged her temple. It might not be a migraine. This was coming on suddenly, more like the flu. That was definitely something neither she nor Gabe needed.

"Hannah? You there?"

"I, um… Yeah. I'm here." She leaned her head against the chair and closed her eyes. "What's up?"

"We need to talk about something. Something big."

"Is it about school?" Why wouldn't her words come out the way she wanted them to? It was as though they thickened in her mouth, sort of like when she was in youth group and they'd played that dumb game where they ate marshmallows and tried to say "Chubby Bunny."

It was a wonder no one had choked to death.

"Are you even listening to me, Hannah?" This time, it wasn't sass in Zoe's voice. It was anger.

Hannah tried to sit up in the chair, but her eyes were getting heavy. "Hey… Something's… I think I'm getting a migraine. Let me call you back." She managed to kill the call and forced herself to stand.

The room rocked, and Hannah grabbed the wall, feeling her way to the bedroom door.

From the living room, Gabe yelled something she couldn't hear. Wasn't he in the basement? Had he called her name?

She staggered into the hall.

The smell of car exhaust slapped her in the face. She stared at the door that led to the garage.

Car exhaust. Gabe's car.

Carbon monoxide.

Where was Gabe?

She stepped toward the den where she thought she'd heard him call to her, but the sudden motion rocked her world…

FIVE

"Hannah!"Gabe yelled, but he couldn't reach her quickly enough.

Her body crumpled as though her skeleton had vanished. She hit the hardwood in the hallway hard.

The house reeked of exhaust. His head pounded. He had to get Hannah into fresh air before both of them dropped and never got up again.

As he made his way to her, he said a silent prayer of thanks that he'd smelled the exhaust fumes before the carbon monoxide reached him. He'd just used the remote start button on his key fob to kill the engine when Hannah came out of her room. Being upstairs on the same level as the garage must have exposed her to more carbon monoxide than had reached the basement. There was no telling how long she'd been breathing in the odorless gas.

By the time he reached her, she'd made it to her hands and knees and was struggling to stand. "We have…to…get out."

"I know." Gabe swooped down, wrapped his arms around her and hefted her to her feet as his own knees threatened to give. "Lean on me. We'll make it. You'll feel better outside."

"Open the windows."

Maybe he should have, but that would waste valuable time and wouldn't wash out the air quickly enough. Both of them needed to get out fast, and they probably needed an ambulance with oxygen.

Patting his pocket to make sure his phone was there, he made his way slowly up the hall, Hannah shuffling beside him, though she was practically dead weight.

This was never going to work.

Bending at the waist tilted the world and made his head ache worse, but there wasn't time to deal with any of that. He swept his hand behind Hannah's knees, cradled her in his arms and headed for the back door off the kitchen.

Hannah tucked her head against his shoulder and mumbled something he couldn't understand. She was fading fast. There was no telling how long the car had been running.

He knew he hadn't left it on, so how had it started all by itself?

No time to worry about that now. He made his way around the corner at the end of the hall and into the kitchen, Hannah growing heavier with each step. "Hang on for me. We're getting outside as fast as we can."

This time, there was no response.

At the door, he managed to get the hand under her knees free enough to turn the deadbolt and pull it open. Gabe stumbled outside, gulping air that didn't feel as though it was coated with oily fumes.

Finally.

Fresh air had never tasted so good.

He laid Hannah on one of the chaises and felt at her throat for a pulse, as if he knew what he was doing. It felt a little fast but was going strong. From what he could remember about his first aid class in college, the cleaner air should help bring her around.

Still, they both needed an ambulance.

He made the call to 9-1-1 and dropped onto the chaise next to Hannah's, the world spinning less with each breath.

His head seemed to pound harder as his thoughts whipped out of control. He knew he'd turned off the car before they went in the house. He always did. If he hadn't, Hannah would have noticed since she entered the garage after him.

Somehow, someone had managed to start his SUV remotely. The vehicle had remote start, but both of the fobs were accounted for. They were sitting on the ledge by the door. He'd used one to turn the car off and the other had been lying beside his wallet.

He dropped his chin to his chest and closed his eyes. *What is going on here, Lord? If You can see everything, how about pointing us in the direction of whoever is doing all of this? My identity is gone. A truck almost hit me...*

The prayer died as quickly as it had started. This went beyond an out-of-control truck in a parking lot or a remote hack into his personal life. No, this hit straight at the heart of his security, of his home. It was a direct attack on not just his physical person, but on his mind and emotions as well.

Why?

On the other chaise, Hannah stirred. For a moment, her unfocused gaze wandered the yard, but then her eyes landed on him and she stopped. "Gabe. Somebody... remoted in and..."

"I know."

She was pale and shivering in the chilled air of an

early spring, mountain night. Her teeth started to chatter, probably because she was dressed in a T-shirt and thin sweatpants and her body was coming out of the shock of oxygen deprivation.

He didn't dare go back into the house for a coat or a blanket, but he couldn't sit by and watch her suffer. He hesitated and then shifted to sit on the edge of her chaise. "Slide over."

She obeyed, and Gabe settled beside her, wrapped his arms around her and pulled her back against his chest. He was warm from fear and from working out, but that probably worked in her favor.

Hannah trembled in his arms. "Thanks." The word was flat and indicated that she knew his actions were out of necessity and nothing more.

If only that were totally true. "No problem." His voice better not have cracked the way he thought it had. There had been a time when he'd wanted nothing more than to hold Hannah like this. To share moments that might have included snuggling under the stars on a spring night.

Dipping his head, Gabe rested his forehead against her hair. Of course, this wasn't anything like he'd once imagined. In the past, when he'd thought about holding her close, it definitely hadn't been because he'd somehow managed to put her life in danger or because she was protecting him from an unseen terror.

In the distance, sirens wailed, approaching quickly, punctuating the surreal night with an eerie sound.

For a moment, Hannah sagged against his chest as her chills subsided.

But she didn't pull away.

As the emergency vehicles drew nearer, casting red-and-white flickers of light against the trees that surrounded the house, she slowly extracted herself from his embrace and sat on the side of the chaise with her back to him. "Thanks. I was…freezing."

It was a necessity, not a moment. He'd do well not to get lost in the same thoughts he'd had about her nine years ago. She was only here because he was in danger, even if they didn't yet know the who and why of it.

Swinging his legs around, he sat beside her, careful not to let their shoulders brush. It was pretty clear she wanted to maintain professional distance. "I'm sorry."

Slowly, as though dizziness still dogged her, she turned her head. "For what?"

"Getting you into this mess."

"*You* got *me* into this mess?" She shook her head and then winced as though it hurt to do so. "No. This is my fault. Somehow, talking to you about this job put someone on your scent."

The job. He'd almost forgotten there had been a job offer on the table. He'd been pretty certain from the get-go that it wasn't something he wanted to do. Now, as paramedics and firemen raced around the house carrying gear, he knew for certain.

If this was the kind of danger and upheaval her career would bring into his ordered world, he wanted nothing to do with it. He'd created a safe life for himself, one that allowed him to do his job and to point out the liars and cheats from behind a screen. He didn't have to look them in the eye. Didn't have to hear their vile words or be the victim of their vile acts.

As a paramedic knelt in front of them, he made his decision. She could keep the job. He wasn't going to do something that would put him—or Hannah—into further danger.

* * *

"Hey!"Hannah called out to the nurse who walked past her cubicle in the emergency room, but the man kept walking.

Sinking against the pillows, Hannah inhaled through her nose, letting pure oxygen do its fabulous work on her brain. The fresh air in Gabe's backyard had already gone a long way toward reviving her by the time they loaded her into the ambulance, but the mask the paramedics had slipped on had made her feel like herself again.

Feeling better meant it was time to get out of here and back to figuring out who was trying to kill Gabe. There was no time for the luxury of lying around like the Queen of Sheba.

The chilled air flooding her sinuses and her lungs was a luxury she'd happily indulge in for a few more minutes. The longer she was hooked up to the stuff, the more she could practically feel the carbon monoxide leaving her body.

She'd been so cold in Gabe's yard, she'd thought her teeth were going to rattle out of her head.

Until Gabe wrapped her in his arms.

The warmth of him had staved off the chill night air battering her skin, but it had brought on a whole new tremor in her chest. One she ought to forget.

A few years earlier, she'd have welcomed an embrace from him. If she'd been reading the signals right back then, he'd probably been ready to offer more than friendship.

If it hadn't been for the investigation into his roommate…

Gripping the sheets in her fists, she forced away any warm-and-fuzzy thoughts. If Gabe ever found out she'd befriended him to get to Trevor, he'd likely never believe that she'd started to fall for him, jeopardizing a federal investigation in the process.

Besides, if she wanted to keep Gabe alive and restore his identity, she had to keep her focus on the target and her heart locked away in the dark closet it had lived in for as long as she cared to remember.

That heart had already gotten her into trouble once. If she'd been paying attention at the house instead of letting herself get distracted by Zoe's phone call, she might have noticed sooner that something was wrong.

She might have rescued Gabe instead of the other way around. It was her job to protect him, and she'd bombed it. Both of them could have died, and their blood would have been on her hands.

No more. From here on out, her focus was 100 percent on the mission.

Two taps sounded on the large window that opened to the main hallway.

Gabe.

He was still dressed in basketball shorts and a moisture-wicking T-shirt. His brown hair looked as though his hand had disrupted it more than once. It was practically standing on end. He looked tired, but as soon as their eyes met, he also looked relieved.

"I heard when I walked by the nurse's station that you're getting out of here as soon as the doctor signs off." He looked over his shoulder and leaned into the room, his hand still braced on the outside of the door frame. "Don't tell anyone I told you that. It probably violates some kind of HIPAA thing." The grin that wrapped around his whisper said he didn't really care.

"I'll keep it to myself." She shifted on the bed and waved him in. "How about you? Since you're up and moving, I'm guessing you beat me in the race to freedom?"

He held up a sheaf of papers as he sat down on the chair at the foot of her bed and propped one leg on the footboard. "I wasn't as exposed as you were, since I was in the basement and you were on the same level as the garage." His expression turned grim, and he toyed with his discharge papers, tearing the edges into fringe. "If I hadn't come upstairs when I did—"

"Stop. It's not your job to protect me."

His eyes flicked to hers, but he went back to tearing the paper as though she hadn't said a thing.

"You're my responsibility. Someone hacking into your car is something that—"

"Should have been on my radar, not yours. I work with tech. My entire house is 'dumb' because of things like that. Houses are completely online, with even ovens accessible by wireless. Everything is an open door for hackers, and I know that. But my car?" He leaned sideways, pulled his cell phone from his pocket, and held it up. "There's an app that will start it remotely. Just because I never downloaded it doesn't mean someone else didn't. The detective I talked to a few minutes ago is convinced that's what happened. He's coming by the house tomorrow to look at the car." He sat up and dropped the papers and the phone onto the foot of her bed then leaned forward, elbows braced on his knees. "I can't do this."

"You can't do what?" she asked. Gabe almost looked tortured. Did he not realize the mistake wasn't his?

He sighed and leaned back in the chair, staring at his feet. "When I was working out downstairs, I started thinking...why not? If there's a bad guy out there who can hack me off the face of the planet, why wouldn't I want to go into a line of work that lets me stop him in his tracks?"

Hannah sat up straighter, the blankets pooling over her sweatpants. "Are you saying you're joining my team?" While it would be hard, and she'd eventually have to tell him the truth, she knew they'd work well together, and he'd do a phenomenal job. Someone with Gabe's abilities would—

"No."

Her excitement deflated as though she was a balloon and his words were the sharpest pin in the sewing box. "Why not?"

"Do you know why I went into cyberpsychology? Why I profile people for a living?" With his papers out of his hands, Gabe had moved on to picking at the threads that held the hem of his shorts together. If he didn't stop soon, he'd have an unraveled mess on his hands, but she was too far away to still his fidgeting.

It wasn't her business anyway. They were his shorts if he wanted to wreck them. Still, she couldn't stand watching him be so unsure of himself.

His continued silence said he was waiting for some sort of acknowledgment. "Why?"

"Because nobody should get to play the victim when they're really the aggressor. Nobody should get to bully their way into a position of authority." His phone buzzed, and he grabbed it from where it rested by Hannah's foot. "In my job now, I can make sure that—" The words died as he scanned the screen. His jaw tightened as he swiped the screen. "You have got to be kidding me."

"Gabe?"

He didn't respond.

This was bad. Hannah sat up, already pulling the

oxygen mask over her head. She gently turned sideways, grateful the world didn't go tilt-a-whirl on her, and scooted down the bed, closer to Gabe's chair. She laid her hand on his wrist and felt how tight his muscles were as he grasped the phone. "What's wrong?"

"It's Trevor." Without looking at her, he passed the phone over.

A blog post from the New Justice Network website was splashed across the screen. A relative newcomer to the scene, the group had hopped onto the online, cold-case bandwagon initially, but they'd shifted in recent months to innocence advocacy, fighting to get a new day in court for incarcerated persons who may have had unfair trials.

According to the post, NJN's latest project involved Trevor Haskell. He claimed that evidence used against him was obtained illegally, because the initial accusations had come from his grad school roommate, who had run an unsanctioned program on his computer.

Gabe was mentioned by name.

Hannah's head jerked up, but Gabe was leaning forward, his elbows on his knees and his fingers clasped at the back of his neck. She'd known from the case file that Gabe had made the initial call to report Trevor. She hadn't known about any computer software.

She started to ask, but Gabe needed a moment to breathe. Not only was he in the crosshairs of someone who didn't want him on an Overwatch team, now he would become the target of hundreds and maybe thousands of people who would claim he'd violated Trevor's rights.

It might be a good thing that his identity had been wiped. At least no one would be able to find him now.

Resisting the urge to rest her hand on his shoulder,

Hannah kept reading. It seemed the program Gabe had used was intended to cull a person's online usage, melding it with observational off-line data to build a comprehensive profile of a subject's personality and likely criminal activities, if any existed. It could even trace markers of mental instability or physical illness by analyzing speech and writing patterns.

Gabe had created something that complex? If this thing was real, it was groundbreaking. The face of profiling and investigations could change with the implementation of such software. Why hadn't he sold it? Used it in his work with Skylark?

She let the phone rest on her knee. Of course, if it worked the way the post hinted it did, it also threw privacy out the window. "That's why you've never talked about it." She muttered the words without meaning to. "Your program is a ticking time bomb."

Gabe sat back in the chair, his face pale. "Exactly. That's why I scrapped it. No one is supposed to know about it. Not even Trevor. How he found out that I stumbled on his extortion while I was testing it is beyond me."

If Trevor wasn't aware of Gabe's involvement, then who leaked the story to NJN? "Who knows you developed this?"

"Only my mentor in grad school, Dr. Donovan Mathison, and he passed away. Initially, I was working on it as part of my doctorate, but we both decided it was a bridge too far, and I moved on to something else."

So he couldn't be the leak. "Do you still have the software?" His name was attached to it, and someone knew it was out there. If the wrong people realized how much they could glean about their enemies, using it—perhaps even ferreting out the manufactured identities of undercover agents or witnesses in WITSEC—Gabe might be in more danger than ever before.

He hesitated before nodding slowly. "There's one copy. In a safe place. Off-line. There was so much work in it that I didn't want to destroy it. I thought that someday I might dial it back and use it, but that never happened. If I could rein it in, someone else could—"

"Unleash it."

SIX

Dawn was softening the horizon when Gabe shoved his front door open and ushered Hannah in. While they'd only been at the hospital a few hours, the ordeal felt like it had lasted lifetimes.

As Hannah slipped past, he pressed himself against the storm door so she wouldn't brush against him. If she did, he might give in to the urge to pull her close again. While that moment on the patio had been about protecting her, the feel of her in his arms had gotten into his head.

Memories had jerked him backward to the time they'd spent together before Trevor had turned her head, when Gabe had thought their friendship could become more.

Now he was having trouble separating past from present. The worst thing he could do was touch her again.

What he ought to do was apologize again. He should have considered that someone could hack his car. It was a concern he'd had before and was one of the reasons he'd never downloaded the remote-start app.

He'd been so frustrated by everything happening around him, so angry with her and with Leigh for basically moving Hannah into his house to keep him safe, as though he couldn't do that for himself…

Obviously, he couldn't. That workout with his earbuds cranked to eleven had nearly cost them their lives.

"Gabe?" Hannah's voice worked its way through his frustration, and he blinked and realized he was standing with one foot in the living room, still holding the door open. Even the ride-share driver who'd just backed out of his driveway was giving him an odd look.

Get out of your head, Buchanan. If someone was looking to sniper him out of existence, he'd just given them the perfect stationary target.

Shutting the door, he flipped the deadbolt and stood awkwardly in the center of his living room. "I'm sorry. I was…thinking." About too many things.

"No worries. I was enjoying the fresh air."

If there wasn't danger around every corner, he'd probably open the windows despite the chill of March in the mountains. Thankfully, his neighbor had aired the place out after the ambulance had pulled away and then locked up behind them. At least the smell of exhaust was gone.

He shuddered a little as he dropped his keys into their spot.

Hannah pointed toward the kitchen. "I was wondering if you had any coffee and if I could make a pot. I got zero sleep in the hospital, and I'm guessing you didn't either."

"Not a bit." He'd been three doors up from her, worried she'd have a seizure and die because someone had targeted him.

At this point, he'd be surprised if he ever slept again, especially with New Justice Network blasting his secrets all over the internet.

How had his life turned into a spy thriller?

He walked through the kitchen where Hannah was filling the coffee carafe with water and straight out the back door he'd carried her through the night before. If he was awake, he might as well watch the day come in. Some of his best prayer times had been on the patio before work. Right now, he could use all of the Jesus time he could get.

Sinking onto the chaise that Hannah had occupied the night before, he turned his face toward the back of his property, which gave way to an open meadow that afforded him views of the mountains through the trees. The sky above was a riot of orange, yellow and red wispy clouds.

It was the perfect display of God's creativity, but the prayers wouldn't come. His head was a muddy mess of words that refused to solidify into anything concrete.

Gabe ran his palms down his basketball shorts, wishing he'd changed into sweatpants but too tired to go inside. Even if Gabe couldn't make words, God heard the jumbled thoughts. His mom had once taught him a verse about the Holy Spirit praying for him when he didn't know how.

He should have listened back then instead of scoffing about Jesus until he'd passed his thirtieth birthday and realized how very much he needed a Savior.

"It's nice out here when you're not actively dying." Hannah's voice came from over his shoulder. She settled on the edge of the other chaise, her knees brushing his arm where it rested on his chair. "You have a great view."

He turned his head toward her, lacking the energy to lift it from the cushion. She was entirely too nonchalant. "You're not out here to talk about my house."

"No. I called my headquarters, and they're sending a couple of agents. I know the police investigated last night and that someone from the department is coming by today, but I still want my people involved. They might see something local law enforcement doesn't."

Gabe bit down on rising frustration. It wasn't like she'd asked.

No, she'd told.

But at the moment, he didn't have it in him to put up a fight. Frankly, the more people involved, the sooner he could have his life back. The sooner Hannah could move out of his guest room and his every waking thought.

She shifted, pressing her knees together and spreading her feet wide, like a little girl on a playground swing set. "I also wanted to see how you're doing with all that's happened with Trevor."

Gabe pressed his palms against his temples and kneaded his scalp, trying to ease the tension that started in his brain and seeped through his body. "It's not Trevor. Not really."

"He never knew you were involved in putting law enforcement on his trail, did he?"

"I didn't think he did." Gabe had been promised that his involvement would be kept confidential, but that was a minor issue. The worst part was he'd felt as though he'd betrayed his roommate. "I never imagined I'd find anything on his laptop that would land him in federal prison."

"What happened?"

There were moments when he still wished he could rewind to that night and never touch Trevor's machine. But then Trevor might not have been caught, and the legislation he'd tried to manipulate Sen. Lacey Chapelle into changing would have been compromised. Trevor would have succeeded in subverting democracy for kicks, just because he could.

There had been nothing to gain. Trevor had simply taken pleasure in terrorizing a senator and manipulating her like a puppet because he held private details about her life. The coldheartedness in the man Gabe had called a friend still sickened him.

"Gabe? What happened?"

Once again, he'd been caught wandering around in his head.

He hadn't talked about that night in years, not since seeking advice from Dr. Mathison and telling his story to the FBI agents at the Charlotte field office. "I was making some changes to the software, working through suggestions from Dr. Mathison. I was also...doubting myself."

"Why?" Hannah leaned forward, seemingly focused on what he was saying, as though she actually cared.

It was tough to remember that she hadn't cared enough to stick around after Trevor's arrest. Hadn't cared enough to be his friend once Trevor had stolen all of her attention. But he still felt the need to unburden himself, especially now, with the bottle shaken to the point of explosion.

"I'd been talking to Dr. M about the ethics of what I was designing, the privacy thing we talked about last night. It was becoming clear that this was bigger than some little program that might help catch a few hackers or cybercriminals." His hesitation hadn't stopped him from pushing forward. He'd been driven by a notion that was relatively new at the time...that online activity could be an indicator of a user's off-line mental or physical state.

If he was being honest with himself, he'd also been

driven by the arrogance of youth and inexperience...
and with the idea of making a name for himself to show
his past tormentors he'd bested them.

Those had been the things that had pushed him one
step too far. "I was toying with the idea that maybe
there wasn't just an internet to search. Maybe with access
to a person's physical laptop, we could learn from
what was on the hard drive."

"Like a third prong?" Hannah's investigative mind
latched on. "Physical interviews, online behavior and
digital content."

Gabe nodded. "I needed to run the program on a laptop
that wasn't mine to make sure there was no bias in
the results. Running it on my own computer wouldn't
let me get that kind of information. I asked Trevor if I
could borrow his laptop, which I did from time to time
because his had better gaming capabilities." The heat
hit the back of his neck. He'd been pretty big into "Call
of Duty" back then.

"But you didn't tell him what you were really doing."

"No, and I got more than I thought I would." He'd expected
to build a routine psychological profile of Trevor.
Instead, the software had uncovered a Pandora's box
filled with emails, photos and texts that had made Gabe
physically ill.

That information had sent him straight to Dr. Mathison
for advice. After the initial shock had worn off for
both of them, Gabe had done the only thing he could do.

With Dr. Mathison at his side, he'd called the FBI.
Only Dr. Mathison ever knew he'd made that call. "I
have no idea how this could have leaked to the New
Justice Network."

"No. But if we find out, that might lead us to who's
after you." Hannah leaned closer, but she didn't touch

him. "This could be one more way to try to hurt you. Outing your program could set any number of people against you. Your saving grace is that no one can find you because you've been scrubbed out of existence."

"Guess they didn't think that through." Small blessing? He wasn't quite ready to call it that.

He had another thing he wanted to discuss anyway. The thing that had eaten at him for too many years. "Why did you disappear when Trevor was arrested?"

He only noticed her hesitation because he was looking at her. If he hadn't been, he never would have known that everything about her froze for the skip of a heartbeat. Probably due to her training, she recovered quickly. "You didn't need me around. You were dealing with losing your best friend after finding out he was a criminal. I figured I'd hurt you enough."

"Maybe I needed you." He hated the way his voice dropped to some kind of romance-movie growl. No way was he going to clear his throat and repeat the words though, because he hated that he'd said them in the first place.

Hannah stood, brushing an invisible something from her dark pants. "I think the coffee's ready." Without meeting his eye, she walked into the house.

Leaving him behind again.

As Gabe stepped onto the front deck with special agent Phillip Campbell to speak to the local police officer, Hannah motioned for Thalia Renner to follow her around the corner into the kitchen, out of sight of the front window.

Tall and athletic, Thalia personified what moviegoers thought Eastern European assassins looked like. Her dark hair and dark eyes intimidated most people, but Hannah had trained the younger federal agent who now worked on a team out of Overwatch headquarters at Camp McGee, about an hour from Gabe's home.

For the next few hours, Thalia and Phillip were on loan to Hannah from Capt. Rachel Blake's team. The two would quietly investigate the carbon monoxide attack after the police were done. At the moment, they were posing as concerned friends. There was no need to let local LEOs know that a top secret investigative outfit was on-site.

"Are you sure you don't want Phillip and me to stay for backup?" Thalia kept her voice low, watching the entryway to the kitchen as though she expected trouble to burst in with guns blazing the moment she let her guard down.

Thalia was a lot like Hannah in that respect. Always on guard. Always protecting. Except today.

Hannah had dropped the ball again, wounding Gabe when she'd walked away without acknowledging his question about Trevor. There were things she couldn't tell him, things that were above any clearance level he currently had. Winding down that road wouldn't help either of them when any answer she gave would be a lie.

"Hannah? Backup? Hello?"

Right. Thalia. "No. The fewer hands we have involved, the better." They didn't need to draw more attention to Gabe. Plus, with Thalia's team leader out on her honeymoon, Overwatch couldn't afford to be two agents down just to pull protection detail.

She should be capable of keeping Gabe safe on her own, though the previous night's events said otherwise.

At the moment, she had more pressing matters. She peeked around the corner to be sure the men were still outside. "I want to run through a few things while there's no risk of Gabe overhearing. I need a sounding board."

Leaning against the dark granite counter, Thalia crossed her arms. "I'm your girl. Let's brainstorm the truth out of this thing."

If Thalia wasn't already happy working on Rachel's team, Hannah would invite her to join the one she was forming. Thalia was a straight shooter who would call someone on an issue faster than she could draw her weapon, but that candidness also came with a wildly sarcastic sense of humor.

Hannah ran through the facts, from the near hit-and-run to the carbon monoxide, keeping one ear tuned to the front door in case the men returned.

"Sounds pretty open-and-shut. Someone wants Gabe Buchanan dead, although wiping him out of every computer out there is strange." Thalia tapped her finger against her forearm. "The obvious question is why you think it's because he talked to you about Overwatch."

"Initially, I did. But now I've got two more suspects to consider." Trevor Haskell and whoever heads the New Justice Network.

"Let me stop you." Thalia dragged the words out as though they carried the weight of her thoughts. "If you stay with the Overwatch thread, this might not be about Gabe at all. It might be about you. Someone could be against you leading a team. Gabe's your first actual recruit."

This was why it was bad to have her emotions involved in a case. Her focus had narrowed to Gabe without any outside considerations.

Still, though it made sense, it wasn't plausible. "I don't know. Few people know we exist, so even fewer people know I'm recruiting. It would have to be someone on the inside. Unless they're out to stalk and torment me by hitting people around me, then the easiest way to stop me from building a team would be to kill me."

"True. Cut off the head, and the beast dies."

"Really? I'm a beast now?"

"In the most respectful of ways." Thalia grinned and then grew serious. "Who else is good for the attacks?"

This was where it got tricky. There were no clear suspects. All she had was hypotheticals. She couldn't even call any of it circumstantial evidence.

Still, she had to run with what she had. "Leigh Lewis is Gabe's partner at Skylark Profiling. I don't have a motive, but she has access to the resources it would take to wipe someone's identity out of digital databases. Although…" Gabe's software might be a motive. If Leigh knew about it, she could want it for herself. Killing Gabe wouldn't make sense in that scenario, unless she had somehow made herself Gabe's beneficiary. It was highly unlikely but worth a look.

"Although what?"

Hannah shook her head. Gabe's software wasn't up for discussion until it needed to be. There was too much she needed to think through. If the motive was obtaining the program, their suspect might be the unknown person who had leaked the information to the New Justice Network.

Thalia crossed her ankles. "Keep your secrets. But I'll bet your next suspect is the roommate who's in jail, Trevor Haskell."

"I'll be visiting the prison if I need to, but Dana's already getting access to his visitor logs and communications. He definitely has the skills to do this. He's also got motive, given that NJN is fighting for him and knows that it was Gabe who turned him in. The only hiccup is that Haskell has zero access to tech. He'd have to have someone on the outside who is as talented as he is."

"Possibly someone in the New Justice Network?" Thalia's eyebrow rose along with the uplift of her voice.

"Possible but not probable. If they're trying to get Trevor freed, the last thing they'd want to do is harm Gabe. If they got caught attacking him, not only would they be on the hook for their own crimes but the assaults would call into question their assertion that Gabe's involvement creates grounds for a retrial."

"So what you've got is nothing."

"What I've got is too much. We haven't even considered a jealous ex or a business rival."

"Or someone out to stop you."

That wasn't very likely, no matter how many times Thalia asserted it was. "We can look into it, but I think it's a waste of resources."

Hannah's phone vibrated in the pocket of the jeans she'd put on after showering away the scent of car exhaust and emergency room.

She glanced at the screen and then held it up to show Thalia before answering on speaker. "Hey, Dana. I'm here with Thalia."

"What's up, ladies?" Dana's greeting was light and breezy, which meant she'd been semisuccessful in finding useful information.

"We're good." That was a lie if Hannah had ever spoken one. If she didn't sleep soon, she'd drop where she stood. A nap for the few hours that Thalia and Phillip were keeping watch would do her wonders. But first, she wanted to hear Dana's intel.

"I can tell by your voice you've found something."

"*Something* can be taken a lot of ways."

"Something *useful*, Dana?"

"You're always challenging me, Austin." She chuckled. "First of all, I have some good news."

Hannah exhaled through pursed lips. "I could definitely use some of that."

"I tracked down Gabe's identity. He's not missing. I mean, a few of his accounts on some less secure servers were deleted or tampered with, but his social and major identifiers were... How can I say this?"

"As plainly as possible." Hannah didn't have the patience for tech stuff. That was why she needed someone like Gabe on her team.

"Okay, it was...masked. Hidden from searches. It's not a very sophisticated hack, and I already undid some of the damage. He has some rebuilding to do, but it won't be as awful as it could've been if he'd been stripped from the system."

Thank you, Lord. Gabe would be thrilled. But clearly, Dana had more. "What else?"

"Well, I'm waiting for the prison to hand over visitor logs, but a contact of mine who knows the ins and outs of the place said it would be tough for Haskell to pass messages without being caught."

"Can you talk to Rich? See if we can justify having Haskell's cell searched? He could be hiding a phone."

Alex "Rich" Richardson ran Overwatch's Camp McGee headquarters. He was the heavy hitter if they wanted something done quickly. Friendly and personable, he could also wield formidable authority when necessary. He got a *yes* faster than anyone else on the team.

He was also Dana's husband. Together, they had a precious toddler who had proverbially wrapped her daddy around her little finger.

"I'll have him call as soon as we get off the phone." A few clicks said Dana was moving on to other info on her computer. "I've been looking into the New Justice Network too. They're a newcomer on the scene, built in the vein of The Innocence Project, helping people who were wrongly convicted." There was an undercurrent to Dana's tone that caused Thalia and Hannah to lock eyes.

"That's admirable." Thalia leaned closer to the phone. "You don't sound like you're impressed."

"I'm impressed with organizations like The Innocence Project. But the New Justice Network? Let's just say they seem to be more about making a name for themselves than they are about actual *justice*."

Hannah gripped the phone tighter. They might be near a lead. "What makes you say that?"

"They were born out of an online group that initially started as a kind of think tank looking into cold cases. You know how that got really big, with conferences and stuff springing up?"

"Still is. Go on."

"Well, NJN took it a step further and started looking into cases where inmates were appealing their convictions. They turned their focus away from cold cases to those."

"Still not seeing a problem." Thalia arched an eyebrow.

Dana exhaled loudly. "Let's put it this way… There aren't a lot of deep-pocket donors when it comes to solving cold cases, but there are a lot of people willing to finance you when you're helping someone find justice."

"Let me guess." Hannah's eyes slipped closed as she started coloring in the picture. "They're choosing high profile or unusual cases, the kinds that will get people talking. The more salacious the better. And they have no regard for whether or not the inmate actually has grounds for a retrial."

"Bingo. And every time they hit on a case, they have a fundraising gala. All cryptocurrency. Hard to follow the money that way. They went public with Haskell's story yesterday, and wouldn't you know it? They're holding a benefit tonight. It involves a silent auction. Crypto only."

"That's definitely shady." Thalia sucked her teeth, her expression turning cold. "There are enough cases of people needing real help. Leeches like this? I'd like to—"

Hannah laid a hand on Thalia's shoulder before she could say something she might regret. "Who's heading up the fundraiser?"

"They have a small board of directors made up of the original online group, and they also have an advisory board I've just started digging into. The chairman of the board is a recent law school grad, Sadie Lawson. Looks like she clerked for a judge in Anson County and then took the job leading NJN."

The front door opened. Gabe's voice, thanking the detective, drifted in.

They needed to end the call.

"Okay. Send me the where and when on their event. I want to be there." While NJN likely wasn't involved in what was happening to Gabe, they might be able to point them to the real culprits. Learning who their source was might be the only thing that kept Gabe alive.

SEVEN

Hannah kept her arm loose where it was tucked into Gabe's elbow. She scanned the large banquet room with floor-to-ceiling windows that looked out over the mountains rolling into the distance. The black halter jumpsuit she wore was a lot more comfortable than the strapless dress Thalia had suggested, but it wasn't her usual attire. The tie on the halter at the back of her neck was a little too tight, aggravating the slight headache that lingered from the previous night's ordeal.

New Justice Network's "little" fundraiser and silent auction had turned out to be a much bigger event than she'd anticipated. The room glowed orange in the sunset light, and it swarmed with North Carolina's elite, including several state senators. Unless her mind was playing tricks on her, the lieutenant governor was in attendance as well.

She really shouldn't have brought Gabe along, but she needed his eyes. If there was anyone at this gala Gabe recognized, it might be a clue as to who had leaked the existence of his software and his part in Trevor's imprisonment. That might lead them to whoever wanted him to suffer.

It was dangerous, but he'd agreed to play along. His

willingness surprised her, given his earlier rant about fighting from behind a screen. Maybe having his secrets dragged into the light had lit a fire under his desire to step into action.

Hannah had wanted to bring Thalia and Phillip along as backup, but Dana had only been able to wrangle two tickets to the gala and silent auction. The other two agents were in a restaurant that was also located in the hotel, on a fake date that looked a bit too much like a real one to Hannah's eyes.

Not that she'd ever say anything to the two of them. Thalia and Phillip were stellar undercover agents who played their parts well. But sometimes chemistry couldn't be denied.

Sort of like the chemistry that hummed between her and Gabe. It had been dampened beneath layers of obligation and past pain, but since he'd held her, the air between them crackled the way it had when she'd first met him.

Especially now, since he was decked out like she'd never seen him before. The black suit, black shirt, and black tie made him look way more mysterious than the man she knew. He was almost a different person.

He was also entirely too tense.

Tugging on his arm, she drew him closer to her side and tipped her head to whisper in his ear as though they were actually a couple. "Whose closet did you raid to find a suit? You look like Sebastian Stan at a movie premiere." With his dark hair and blue eyes, that wasn't actually far from the truth.

Some of the tension released from Gabe's shoulders. With his head tipped down toward hers and his gaze focused ahead of him, he smiled slightly, adding to the charm.

Hannah almost shivered. *Yep. There was a lot of chemistry.*

Turning his head slightly, he brushed her ear with a whisper. "I have a church buddy who's the same size as me and plans weddings for a living."

The warmth of his breath sent a quiver into Hannah's stomach that proved to be a little bit too distracting. If she turned toward him even a little—

"Anything good happening over there?" Thalia's voice came through her earpiece, jolting Hannah back into reality.

She pulled away and straightened. Thalia's timing was, as usual, spot-on. "Nothing yet."

Gabe's grip on her arm tightened, keeping her close to his side, probably at the hint that there was someone in Hannah's ear. It was a stark reminder of the reason they were at this gala. His smile faded.

This was not his wheelhouse at all. No matter how much he'd assured her he could hold up under the pressure, she needed to remember this was the first time he'd ever been in a position like this.

"You're doing great." She slid her arm through his grasp until she could lace her fingers with his and give him a gentle squeeze.

Support. She was only holding his hand for support.

When he glanced down at her, it was clear he was trying to relax.

Trying and failing.

"All I can think is that there might be someone here who knows things about me, but I don't know them. It's like somebody is looking into my brain without permission."

"They're not. Whoever is doing this, they person-ally knew you at some point. Maybe they overheard you talking to your professor one day. Or maybe Trevor knew more all along than you thought he did." That wasn't plausible, because if he'd been aware before, that Gabe's software was behind the investigation, he'd have used the information in his first trial. Still, if it eased some of Gabe's fears...

He nodded slowly, his fingers tight around hers. "So I'm looking for anyone I might know or even slightly recognize?" His voice held a thin edge.

"Yes, but if you see someone, do whatever you can to keep them from seeing you."

"Whatever you say."

Hannah spotted a waiter carrying champagne glasses and waved him over. It might help Gabe to have something to do with his hands. "Do you have anything non-alcoholic?"

The young man nodded and glanced at Gabe. "Wait here." Clearly, even he could feel Gabe's discomfort. The waiter was back in under a minute. "Sparkling water with fresh peaches."

Hannah pulled her hand from Gabe's and mouthed a thank-you to the young man, who passed her two drinks, one wrapped in a napkin. He winked at her before he walked away.

She looked down, curious.

Yep. There was a phone number on the napkin.

Seriously? She pressed the note against the sweating glass, letting condensation blur the numbers. Being hit on was never fun, and it was less fun when the guy throwing winks around was supposed to believe she had a date on her arm.

She passed one of the glasses to Gabe and sipped hers, searching faces. From their vantage point at the side of the room, they could see a large cross section of the guests, though the glare of sunset made a few faces tough to discern. She nudged Gabe farther toward the middle of the wall, to a tall table where they could stand and look a bit more casual.

She slipped to the back of the table, close to the wall, drawing Gabe with her. "Stand here. With the wall behind you and the table in front of you, you'll feel less exposed." It was a psychological trick she'd learned when she was first studying undercover tactics. Simple but effective.

Gabe smiled gratefully and stood where she indicated. After a moment, he seemed to breathe easier.

Hannah stayed close, just a couple of inches away, almost touching, but not quite. They were supposed to look like a couple, and that meant playing the part.

After a moment, he rested both hands on the table, relaxing slightly. "I'm a lot more comfortable in blue jeans than in Brendan's suit."

"Well, it looks good on you."

"Like I'm playing Sebastian Stan at a movie premier?" His eyes sparkled and he sipped his drink. "You said it earlier, but it also seems you told me something to that effect back when we were binge-watching Marvel movies once."

Heat hit Hannah's cheeks, and her lids slipped down. Yes, she had said that back in the day. Although she'd never mentioned her crush on the Winter Soldier, it seemed Gabe wasn't clueless about it.

He smiled around his drink and then settled it on the table. "I didn't know women blushed after the age of thirty."

She tilted her head to the side. "Are you flirting?"

"Aren't I supposed to be?" A flicker of uncertainty narrowed his eyes, but then he matched her head tilt, suddenly looking totally at ease with the role he was playing. "Did you know I was a drama geek in high school?"

"Were you?"

"Yep." He nodded and scanned the crowd. "Ensemble in *Guys and Dolls*." He leaned closer and whispered near her ear. "Also requiring a suit." As he pulled away, his cheek brushed hers.

Hannah's breath caught in her throat. As it turned out, a relaxed Gabe was a much bigger threat than a tense one.

He cleared his throat and went back to watching the guests. His left hand was shoved into his pants pocket while his right slowly rocked his glass back and forth on the table. "I still don't understand this. The day before yesterday, I was just a guy who tapped on a keyboard for a living, digging into people's lives from the outside."

Digging into people's lives... They had more than enough motives and suspects already, almost too many, but he'd just offered more.

"Is there a possibility someone lost out on a job because you uncovered something while building their profile?"

He seemed to read the air before he finally shook his head. "Doubtful. Few people know what company did their background checks, let alone who the specific employee was. Even if they did figure out it was Skylark, they'd have a tough time connecting the dots to me. Leigh is the face of the company."

"But you're the only profiler on staff."

"That's true." Low conversations and laughter ebbed and flowed around them as the two hundred or so people in the ballroom chatted in small groups or perused the silent auction tables that dominated the far side of the room. "Still, my name isn't out there. Anyone looking would have to dig deep to find it."

Apparently, someone had dug, because they'd been able to wipe his identity. They were bound to know where he worked.

Gabe's glass thunked flat on the table, sloshing flavored water onto his hand. He didn't seem to notice.

"What?" Hannah edged closer, her arm pressing against his. No one seemed to be paying any attention to them, and no face sparked alarm bells.

Slowly, Gabe turned, blocking her view of the room. He looked down at her, his eyes wide. "Quentin Fisher. Over my left shoulder, near the sculpture by the front window. Brown hair. Navy suit. He can't know I'm here, but he's walking this way."

Wow. She was almost impressed with his summary of the situation. "Follow my lead." She couldn't look like they'd seen anything out of the ordinary. Leaning closer to Gabe, she laid her hand flat on his chest and acted as though she was whispering in his ear as she spoke to Thalia. "Dig into Quentin Fisher. He works with Gabe at Skylark." Gabe's heart rate accelerated against her palm as Hannah scanned the room over his shoulder, gaze landing on a man in a navy blue suit, standing halfway between the sculpture and their position, staring at her.

She looked past him as though she hadn't noticed. "He's watching us." She pulled away slightly, but Gabe slipped his arms around her waist, drawing her closer and trapping her hand against his chest.

What is he doing?

"Make him think we're together, right?" His voice held a low rumble she'd never heard before. His blue eyes latched on to hers, scanning her face from forehead to mouth. Beneath her palm, his heart rate accelerated.

Hers probably raced too. But while his was reacting to the threat to his life, hers was definitely a response to him.

Especially when he dipped his head and rested his forehead against hers. "I'm not sure I can do this."

Neither was she. Because if he came any closer, she might tear down every wall she'd ever built between them, ignoring the danger that the outside world posed to him...

And that Gabe posed to her.

He really couldn't do this.

Somewhere behind him was a coworker who may or may not have tried to erase his record and then tried to kill him. That should be occupying his attention.

But just as she had all night, Hannah kept taking up residence in every thought and action. She'd walked out of his guest room earlier wearing a dressed-up, black, one-piece pantsuit thing that tied around her neck, looking like...

Well, like something he didn't have words for. Her red hair was tied up in some kind of knot at the back of her head with wispy pieces around her face and brushing her nape.

He'd been fighting the urge to take this game to the next level and to plant a kiss right where her neck met her shoulder. Nothing too out of control. But it was still definitely something he shouldn't do.

She was making him crazy. The whispering in the ear and the pulling him closer as though they did this every day. As though she had a right to be near him.

As though he had a right to be near her.

It was a right he'd always wanted. The right to be the guy who brushed her hair back or kissed her cheek or held her hand. Now she was in his arms, her lips a literal breath from his…

And it was all an act.

Part of him didn't even care. He could kiss her the way he'd always wanted to, could take this one chance to know how it would feel…

But it would be so wrong.

They stood face-to-face for a long moment, breath to breath, in an excruciating dream world. She brushed her lips against his so lightly that he almost didn't feel it, then rested her chin on his shoulder.

Gabe's eyes slipped shut. For half a second, he could pretend—

"He stopped watching. He's wandered off to look at one of the auction tables."

Bubble burst. Dream over.

Trapped between Hannah and the table, Gabe opened his eyes and stared at the black curtain that draped the wall. He dropped his arms from her waist as she backed away. He could breathe again, but he wasn't sure he wanted to. Twice now, he'd held her. Twice, he'd forgotten that this wasn't past dreams come true.

This was life or death.

He shoved his hands into his pockets as she watched the room over his shoulder. "Should we go?" *Please?* He wanted track pants and the sanctity of his gym, somewhere silent where he couldn't feel her breathing.

The room was stifling, and he had to almost physically wrestle down the urge to pull his collar away from his throat.

Hannah didn't look at him as the crowd's conversations broke over him in crashing waves. The noise wasn't loud, but it was a consistent buzz that hummed in Gabe's brain until he couldn't think.

Maybe that was the problem. He wasn't thinking straight because there was too much stress and too many people. He'd had social anxiety ever since the bullying started in middle school, but he'd managed to bottle it up as he grew older.

It roared back in with a vengeance now. The threats on his life… The presence of a woman who reminded him of his failures…

If he didn't get out of this room soon, he'd break the table in half. He balled his hands into fists inside his pockets and tried to hold on.

Hannah laid a warm hand on his arm. "You're so tense I can feel it over here. Look at me."

Absolutely not. She was the problem. Well, she was half of the problem. Feeling like a sniper had him in crosshairs was the other half.

He really wasn't sure which was worse.

She let go of his arm, pulled his left hand from his pocket and bumped something cool and damp against it. "Drink this."

He guzzled sparkling water so fast that his throat burned. The pain jolted his thoughts back into line. "What now?"

She handed him her drink as well. "Quentin Fisher left."

"Are you talking to me or Thalia?" He was having trouble tracking who her words were directed to when she had an invisible friend in her ear.

"Both of you." She tipped her head to one side, listening. "Phillip, he headed out the main doors. Keep an eye on his movements."

That was probably code for "Make sure he doesn't plant a bomb in our vehicle."

Hannah plucked a gilded card from a stand in the center of the table and scanned it, then she looked at him. "Can you hold on for a bit longer? Sadie Lawson is going to formally open the evening, and I want to see if we can get a read on her."

"She's the head of NJN?" He wanted to see her too. According to the byline on the NJN website, she'd penned the post that named him. While he preferred to fight his battles from a distance, he couldn't turn down an opportunity to look his enemy in the face. "I can wait."

While Hannah flagged a waitress for more drinks, Gabe leaned an elbow on the table and tried to look at ease as he watched the crowd.

He also watched for the first waiter. The guy had slipped Hannah a phone number that she'd promptly destroyed. That little act of loyalty to him brought on the same kind of roller coaster in his stomach that holding her in his arms had.

It shouldn't.

He forced himself to focus on the task and not on the woman beside him. "Why was Quentin here?"

She said nothing as a waitress approached and settled two more sparkling waters in front of them. A few beats after the young woman walked away, Hannah faced him, mimicking his pose with her elbow on the table.

He noticed she kept her distance. "I don't know. It's likely his presence is a coincidence. He could believe in what NJN stands for. He could be here with a date. We'll dig in and check him out. But here's a question…" She laid a hand on his arm as though she was flirting with him, still playing the game. "You profile people for a living. Anything stand out about Quentin Fisher?"

"I vetted him before he came on, but that was several years ago. He tends to keep to himself. He's a tech guy. Loves machines more than people. He's been with Skylark almost since the beginning. Nothing stands out."

"You never asked him for help with your software?"

"No. Although…" This was one of those moments when he literally wanted to smack himself in the head. He should have thought of it before, but so much had happened so fast, the incident had flown right out of his brain. "Before you came in yesterday, there was a comment made at work."

"By Quentin?"

"No. By Leigh." It should have jolted him more at the time and would have…if his identity hadn't vanished in the same instant. "Right before you came in with your off-the-Richter-scale earthquake, she asked about my software."

"Wait." Hannah straightened and jerked her hand from his arm as the lights dimmed and the crowd quieted. She dropped her voice to a whisper. "How did she know?"

A female voice from the stage stopped him from replying. "Welcome, ladies and gentlemen. I'm Sadie Lawson, the chairman of the board of the New Justice Network. Thank you for attending our Mission Possible Gala!"

Applause exploded in the room.

On a small stage at the back of the ballroom, a woman in a red dress held the audience's attention. Long brown hair spilled over one shoulder. She was shorter and younger than Gabe had expected, even though he knew she was fresh out of law school. Something about her high-energy presence was captivating. At least for the audience. For him, that bright smile didn't sit right.

"She's as fake as her acrylic nails," Hannah muttered.

Gabe swallowed a chuckle. Guess she saw it too.

The giant screen behind Sadie came to life, and photos of smiling men and women flashed by, hugging families or giving a thumbs-up to the camera.

Sadie gestured to the images. "As many of you know, over the past three years, NJN has helped nearly two dozen wrongly convicted men and women find justice and transition back into life in society. It's because of your donations that we've been able to do such amazing work." She went on to talk about a man named Josiah Utley, who'd been cleared of an embezzlement conviction.

Hannah leaned closer. "This sounds more like a multilevel marketing pitch than a nonprofit fundraiser." Her eyes reflected the changing lights of the screen. "She's taking a good thing and making it feel…"

"Slick? Packaged?"

"Yeah. And people are eating it up."

"She's charismatic." It was hard not to be drawn in as Sadie spoke with passion about justice and fairness.

"At NJN, we've just taken on our most ambitious project yet." The screen behind Sadie went dark, dropping the room into dramatic shadows.

Beside him, Hannah scoffed beneath her breath. "Showmanship."

When the screen burst back to life with Trevor's mug shot dominating the space, it was like a bomb hit the room. Gabe gripped the edge of the table at the sudden smack of recognition. Easing closer, Hannah slipped her arm around his waist as though she could support him.

This time, he knew her touch was no act. Few people

realized that Gabe had lost his best buddy with the rev-elation of Trevor's crimes, and that he still dealt with the emotional fallout of having trusted a criminal with his friendship.

But Hannah knew.

Sophie's voice droned on, buzzing in his brain. "Trevor Haskell was a graduate student at Blue Ridge University when he was accused and later found guilty of bribing a public official, among other charges. How-ever, NJN has learned that the informant who initially turned him in was his roommate, who violated Trevor's privacy by running unauthorized software on his com-puter. The existence of this software should horrify any-one who believes in the right to privacy. Additionally, NJN believes it was actually that roommate, Gabriel Buchanan, who is guilty of the bribery Trevor is cur-rently serving time for."

Gabe nearly shouted the word *liar* before Hannah's grip around his waist tightened.

"I've heard enough." Hannah tugged him toward the closest exit, which was only a few feet away. "Let's go."

Sophie's voice followed them to the door. "Inter-estingly, all traces of Gabriel Buchanan vanished on the same day that NJN went public with our intention to help Trevor Haskell. If that doesn't speak of guilt, what does?"

The crowd murmured. He heard his own name more than once now.

Gabe turned back as the screen changed again, this time to a photo of him with Trevor and Hannah in grad school. The same one from his now-missing, once-private social media account.

Hannah gasped and stopped walking.

"We need your help—" Sophie's voice grew stron-

ger, more determined, more pleading "—to free Trevor
Haskell and to bring the man who might be the real
criminal, Gabriel Buchanan, to justice."

EIGHT

"Are you kidding me?" If Hannah had carried a clutch to the gala, she'd have hurled it across Gabe's living room as she walked inside. When Thalia had brought her the pantsuit, Hannah had joked that it had pockets.

She couldn't take her frustration out on pockets.

Gabe, Thalia and Phillip were behind her, so she couldn't even slam the door.

Instead, she opted to smack her palms onto the granite bar that separated the dining area from the kitchen. She'd held her anger all the way back to the house, but now it refused to be contained.

"I want everything we can dig up on Sadie Lawson." She turned toward her makeshift team. "Right now."

"I'll call Dana." Phillip headed for the guest room where Hannah was bunking.

Thalia stood with Gabe near the couch. With her arms crossed over her stomach, she tapped her index finger on her biceps, studying Hannah with a practiced eye.

Gabe's jaw was tight, and the furrows in his forehead were deep. He hadn't spoken since they left the gala. Without making eye contact with either of them, he loosened his tie and stalked up the hallway. The door to his room closed seconds later.

Hannah dropped her chin to her chest. She shouldn't have blown up like that, but her insides were a shaken soda bottle. Once they were back in the relative safety of Gabe's house, the lid had blown.

More than anything, she wanted to tell Gabe they would fix this, but at every turn, the situation spun more out of control. She was failing him, Overwatch…

"Are you done pitching a hissy fit like Rich and Dana's two-year-old?" Thalia's voice was low, with no trace of amusement.

What remained of Hannah's anger evaporated, sapping her energy. Pulling out one of the iron bar stools, she sank onto the edge and fingered the dangling end of the fabric belt that tied at her waist. "It's like, the more we find out, the more we don't know. And now Gabe is…" She fluttered her hand toward his room. "It was bad enough that Sadie Lawson publicly posted his name and the existence of his software on a blog, but to out him that way in public?" She shook her head. Whatever this was, it was growing more dangerous by the moment. "She convicted him without a trial tonight. Why? What is the point of making Gabe look like a criminal?"

"It casts doubt on Trevor Haskell's conviction if there's another viable suspect. The more of a groundswell of public support she can start, and the more she can turn a spotlight on Gabe, the more likely she is to get a new trial for Trevor."

"Gabe ought to sue her for slander." It would be tough to win though. The "we believe" and the "who might be" that she framed her accusations with twisted her statements into opinions, which were protected by free speech.

The woman was slick.

"So what's really going on with you?" Thalia leaned back against the door, still watching. Knowing her, she was trying to read Hannah's thoughts. "This is not team leader behavior."

That comment should have lit every fuse Hannah had, but she tamped down the flame. Thalia was right. If Hannah was going to take charge of a team, she couldn't pop off like a toddler who'd been denied her fish-shaped crackers.

She paced to the blank TV and studied her muted reflection. All decked out in semiformal attire with her hair pulled up, she definitely didn't look like herself. Nor did she feel like herself.

"I can usually put things together in logical sequences, but this case? It's like someone handed me a paint-by-number set, only there are no numbers on the paint pots. And every time I think I've figured out which color goes where, someone switches the picture."

"Or steals your paintbrushes." Phillip walked into the room, pocketing his phone as he nodded toward Thalia. "We have to go."

"What?" Hannah had known they weren't staying long, but this was abrupt.

Thalia neatly caught the backpack Phillip tossed to her, already turning toward the door. "What's up?"

"There's a break in the baby-smuggling case. We're being briefed at midnight by a contact out of Moldova." He tilted his head with a gleam in his eye. "Want to get married?"

Hannah looked from one to the other. What in the world was going on?

Thalia turned back toward Hannah, shouldering her backpack. "We've been prepping for the possibility of going undercover as a married couple. Looks like the honeymoon is starting." She reached for the door. "Sorry to ditch you."

"Actually, we're not ditching you right away." Phillip hesitated as he ushered Thalia out the door. "We can catch some sleep at HQ after the briefing and be back first thing in the morning. Rich says there are logistics to put together, and we have a few days to support you if you need us."

Hannah tried not to melt with relief. With Gabe's case changing by the second, she really didn't want to be without backup.

"Dana is checking into Sadie Lawson and will call you," Phillip said. "As for your paint-by-numbers problem, I think your next logical step is to visit Trevor Haskell in prison. He's likely the one holding the color key."

She'd already considered that, along with a dozen other people she needed to interview.

Phillip smiled. "I know what it's like to get in the weeds so deep that you need somebody to point the way so you can think clearly again. It happens. Especially on a case like this one. I'll be praying for you guys." He tipped his chin as a goodbye and closed the door behind him.

"If you go see Trevor, I'm going with you." Gabe's voice came from the hallway.

Hannah whirled on him. "Seriously? What is with you guys and sneaking up on me?"

Holding his hands aloft in mock surrender, Gabe walked into the room and sat on the stool Hannah had vacated. He'd changed into basketball shorts and a gray T-shirt.

If Hannah had to guess, she'd say he was about to

head to his basement to work off some of his anxiety and frustration.

She should probably join him.

Also, he was not going with her to the prison. "I can't let you do that."

Shrugging, Gabe rested his hand on the granite counter and drummed his fingers. "I can go with you, or I can go on my own. There's nothing to stop me from visiting Trevor if I want."

Technically, she could request a hold on Haskell's visitation, but that would require navigating the court system, and she didn't have that kind of time. If Gabe was determined to go, she'd rather he not take off alone. He'd backed her into a corner.

"Fine, but I talk. You listen. If he acts for one second like he's got a grudge against you or might be behind this, then—"

"Then I will leave quietly."

"Don't forget that promise." She took in his slouched shoulders and his still-tight expression, and her professional thoughts melted. Gabe was a man in pain. "You holding up okay?"

He shrugged. "It's a lot at once."

"And a lot of it makes no sense. I think—" Her phone vibrated in her pantsuit pocket, the rhythm she'd customized for her sister. As much as she hated to ditch Gabe, this was Zoe, and too many things had been left unsaid on their last call. "I should take this. I was on the phone with my sister before we had to go to the hospital. I sent her a text that all was well, but I'm sure she's looking for more confirmation." As Hannah herself would be under the same circumstances.

Actually, she'd have beaten the ambulance to the hospital if Zoe had been inside.

Gabe waved her off. "I'll be in the basement."

Hannah watched him walk away, torn between family and…and Gabe. Finally, she pressed the phone to her ear. "Hey, Zoe." She headed up the hall toward her room. Pajamas were on the agenda. "What's up?"

"I'm sorry I didn't call earlier today to see how you're doing, but things were…busy."

Something in Zoe's tone was off. Hannah stopped at the door and pressed the phone tighter to her ear as she flipped on the bedroom light. "What kind of busy—"

"Are you really okay? I mean, I got your text and you said you were, but I wanted to be sure. Carbon monoxide is no joke. Was it an accident? Are you on a dangerous case? Should I be worried?" The sentences mashed together into one long thought without a breath in the middle.

Either Zoe was scared or there was something else going on. Hannah sank to the edge of the bed and kicked off the black heels she'd hated from the moment she slipped them on. "First, I'm fine. Second, you know I can't talk about my job. And third…what's really going on with you? I can tell something's up. I practically raised you, remember?"

"You never let me forget."

Well, that was definitely a tone. "What does that mean?"

"Never mind." Zoe's sigh carried the long-suffering weight of her college-student angst. "We need to talk about something."

Suddenly, the little girl Hannah had *practically raised* sounded like a very mature young woman.

This was much scarier than being poisoned with carbon monoxide. Hannah had worked her entire life to make sure Zoe and Eli were protected and that Zoe had the money she needed for school. She'd fought to keep her siblings safe, fed and loved, to give them a stable life in an unstable situation.

Something in her gut said that Zoe was about to rock that foundation. "What's going on?"

"Eli is at Fort Bragg in the Q Course." The words rushed out of Zoe in one breath.

"What?" The Army's qualification course for Special Forces? "Is he out of his mind? Why wouldn't he tell me?" Hannah's heart pounded. Her baby brother, going toe-to-toe with terrorists and worse on some of the deadliest missions in the world? "What is he thinking?"

"He told me to wait to tell you until he was there and you couldn't stop him. And your reaction is why."

Zoe couldn't be serious. "My reaction? Does he not realize how dangerous this is?"

"Eli is a grown man, Hannah. He's twenty-three and a sergeant in the Army. I think he knows how to weigh the risks."

"But…" In the distance, a car horn blared. A dog in a nearby yard barked. Normal world sounds shouldn't be happening when her security was ripping apart. "Eli was supposed to take a job that kept him relatively safe." She'd tried to steer him toward logistics.

"I'm not even going to dignify what you just said with a response, Miss Carbon Monoxide."

That was different. That was…herself. The thought of Eli not only running into danger but running into the world's *worst* danger? That was—

Zoe's heavy sigh stopped further thought and amped Hannah's suspicions. "Something tells me there's more to this than Eli, Zo."

"There is. And it's a good thing."

"You don't sound like it." She sounded more like the way she had when she was five and her pet goldfish, Rocket, died.

"Because I don't want to hear what you're going to say."

Did her siblings really dread telling her news, good or bad, out of fear of her reactions? "Well, it can't be worse than your brother hurling himself in front of bullets and bombs."

"Like you do?" Before Hannah could answer, Zoe charged forward. "Enough of that. I just called to tell you that…" She inhaled deeply and then spoke in a rush. "Hannah, last night, I got married."

"Buckle your seat belt." The car rocked as Hannah slammed the driver's-side door after barking the command.

Gabe settled his soda into the cupholder by his knee and kept his mouth shut. Snapping back wouldn't help whatever was going on with her.

They'd left his house at sunrise and had been on the road for over an hour. They'd stopped at a gas station outside Sulfur Springs to fuel up and give Phillip and Thalia, who were trailing them by about half an hour, time to catch up.

Gabe shifted in the passenger seat and stared at Hannah, literally biting his tongue. Whatever had happened on that call from her sister, it had lit a fire in her. It had kept her silent for most of the car ride, but it also had her taking some of the curves on their route through the mountains a little faster than his stomach would like.

Worse, her attitude grated on his nerves like a computer fan that refused to shut off. She'd bossed the life out of him since breakfast. Had even said something about the amount of coffee he poured into his travel mug. *You should cut back on the caffeine. You'll never sleep at night.*

In what might go down as the wisest move of his life, he hadn't said a word about the monster cup of coffee she was fixing for herself at the time. Or the large cup she'd just purchased.

Pushing the start button, she glared at him. "Well?"

"Well, what?"

"You going to buckle up?"

Gabe slipped his thumb between the seat belt and his chest, pulled it forward and let it snap back.

Working her jaw as though she was chewing on her next words, Hannah reached for the gear shift.

Something was wrong, and if Gabe didn't intervene in the next ten seconds, he'd either bite back at her or he'd have to endure the roller coaster that was her angry driving style.

He really didn't want to yell or lose his breakfast. Despite his better judgment, Gabe laid his hand on hers. "Stop a second."

There was a hesitation before Hannah pulled away, but it wasn't fast enough to prevent the warmth of her hand from reminding him of what it had felt like to hold her.

She ran her knuckles along her denim-clad thigh as though she'd felt it too and could somehow erase his touch. "We need to get moving. The prison knows we're coming, but we have a set window of time to interview Trevor."

"We still have a cushion."

She whipped her head toward him. This impulsive version of Hannah, with her feelings written all over her face, was more disconcerting than Gabe wanted to admit. While she normally kept her feelings close to the vest, emotions were practically seeping through her skin now.

He shrugged. "I heard you talking to Thalia about our schedule." He wasn't going to apologize for eavesdropping when she'd left the bedroom door open as she spoke on the phone. "But that's not what has you jumpy. What's going on with your sister?"

"With my— What makes you think there's something going on with my sister? Or that my family is open for discussion?" She rested her hand on the gear shift and angled in the seat so she could back out of the parking space.

Gabe gently curled his fingers around her hand and lifted it.

This time, she didn't pull away.

No way was he going to acknowledge how that made his heart feel. "Look, we used to be friends. Clearly, something is bothering you. Considering how deep you're into my personal life right now, you might as well share a little of yours." He squeezed her fingers. "And I'm aware you're a federal agent and I'm just a civilian, which normally wouldn't lend itself to you spilling your guts, but I'd like to think I'm a more than just a case to you." Especially after that spark had flared up between them at the gala.

Yeah, he'd promised himself he wasn't going to think about that.

Staring out the windshield at the white cinderblock gas station, Hannah almost seemed to count to ten before she spoke. "If we can get moving so I don't feel like we're sitting here being a stationary target, I'll talk."

Gabe released her hand and pulled his back to rest on his knee. "Fair enough. Keeping us alive is a smart idea." It felt weird being the calm one. Something must really be getting to Hannah for her to be so out of sorts.

She didn't speak again until they were several miles down the road. She'd chosen to take the back route where a tail would be easier to spot. They followed the winding two-lane road through the mountains, glimpses of rolling peaks and valleys visible through the trees. "I'll feel a lot better once Thalia and Phillip are tucked behind us."

So would Gabe.

Hannah drove with both hands on the wheel, navigating curves and straightaways as though she'd been trained by NASCAR, although she drove the speed limit, probably allowing time for the other two to catch up.

"Everything is out of control. This investigation, my brother and sister, you." She waved a hand up and down as though encompassing his entire existence.

Interesting that she viewed him as one of the things she couldn't control. "Me?"

"The things that are happening to you, I mean." She shifted her grip on the wheel and settled into her seat, stretching her arms. "My sister eloped."

It took a second for the conversational shift to register. "As in, she got married? Isn't she in college?"

Hannah nodded. "At Brevard. She's studying criminal justice."

"And she just up and married a guy? Do you even know him?" It wasn't unheard of to get married in college. It wasn't necessarily a bad thing either, but something about Hannah's demeanor said it might be the end of the world. "Do you not like the guy? Is he trouble?"

"It's not that. They've been dating since they were

in ninth grade. Kevin is a great guy. Super responsible. He's a welder and already has a nice career going."

"So he's a good person, and it's not about money?" Sure, marriage was a big step, especially at a young age, but everyone lived their lives differently.

"No, it's…" Again with the hand wave. "She should have finished college first."

"She's dropping out?" Okay, that could be a problem.

"No. She should have waited." The words cracked like a whip.

Gabe drummed his fingers on the window ledge and watched the trees breeze by, thankfully slower than they had earlier. However, if the way she spit those words out was any indication, Hannah might bear down on the gas again and make him wish he'd indulged in anti-nausea meds before they hit the road.

He really couldn't see a problem with a marriage in school. It happened. Several of his friends had walked down the aisle while in college or immediately after. Most of them were doing fine. For a couple who had been together as long as her sister and her new husband had been, it didn't sound like an awful thing.

He didn't dare say that out loud though. The next time, her words might cut. "Is there…anything else?"

Her sharp exhale said there was. Hannah glanced in the rearview and then in the side mirrors. "Zoe also dropped the bomb that our brother, Eli, is in the Q Course at Bragg."

"You'll have to explain that to me."

"Qualification course for Special Forces. You know, the best of the best. High stakes. High danger." Her voice took on a tension Gabe had never heard before.

So this was the real problem. Her brother was about

to run headlong into danger that Hannah couldn't protect him from.

Hang on a second. That's what all of this was about. She'd mentioned being out of control. She couldn't control her siblings, and it was gutting her.

He studied her, settling into profiler mode. Given what she'd shared about her background in the past, control was a big issue with her. Bigger than she likely realized. With a father who'd worked third shift and an absentee mother, Hannah had been a parental figure. She'd spent her life trying to protect her siblings. As her brother and sister moved forward in theirs, doing adult things and making adult decisions, she was losing control of them. They were flying, and she could no longer take charge of how they set their wings to take to the skies.

"What are you thinking?" Hannah glanced at him and then back to the road. "I can hear your brain ticking."

Given her mood, he wasn't about to tell her he'd been analyzing her. "I'm just listening. You seem—"

A strange *whomp-whomp* started out low and grew in intensity, filling the SUV's cabin with a sound he'd heard—and hated—before.

"Flat tire." Muttering under her breath, Hannah lifted her foot from the gas and slowed the vehicle. She scanned the side of the road, which dropped off quickly into a ravine and trees. Her sigh was heavy.

"Thought so." Gabe pointed to a straight stretch as they exited the turn. "There's a turnoff for a driveway or something."

"I see it." She eased the car onto what was actually a gravel service road with a gate across it and then shut off the engine. "Stay here. I'll check the tire, see what we're dealing with." She slammed the door behind her.

No way was she changing a tire by herself. He had too much chivalry in him to allow for that. Gabe climbed out of the car and walked down the side of the vehicle. The rear passenger tire was puddled on the gravel. There was no filling that with canned air. They were going to have to bust out the jack and the spare.

But…where was Hannah?

Gabe stepped to the back of the vehicle and found her staring up the road instead of setting up the jack. "What's going on?"

She shook her head. "There was a red pickup behind us just before the tire went flat."

"Okay?"

"Where is he?" She pursed her lips and shook her head, still watching the curve. "He wasn't that far behind, so he should have passed us by now."

Gabe hadn't noticed a vehicle, but he also hadn't been watching the way Hannah had been trained to. "Maybe he turned on a side road or into a driveway?"

"No. For the past few miles, there's been rock face to the left of us and ravine to the right. This is the first place that's been wide enough to pull off." She rested a hand on the pistol at her hip. "No other cars have come by either."

The worry in her tone crawled up his spine. "What do you think—"

"Get back in the car. Now." Hannah shoved him around the vehicle. "I don't like—"

The back window shattered as a gunshot echoed off the mountain.

NINE

Hannah drew her SIG as she shoved Gabe around the vehicle. "Are you hit?"

"No."

With a brief prayer of thanks, Hannah edged backward, closer to the front of the SUV, forcing Gabe to back up as well. She passed her phone to him. "Unlock code is 9204. Call Thalia. Share our location and tell her what's happening."

She scanned the road and the ravine. That shot hadn't come from above, so the shooter was on their level. But where? Aside from the breeze, nothing moved among the trees.

As Gabe spoke to Thalia, Hannah tried to listen for twigs cracking. If she had to guess, the shooter had been behind the wheel of that red pickup, and they'd blocked the road with their vehicle. Otherwise, another car would have come by already.

Obstructing the road would bring the police, but it would also jam up the works long enough for the shooter to pursue and destroy.

Hannah tightened her grip on her pistol. *Not today.*

Gabe ended the call and tapped the phone on her shoulder.

Hannah shook her head. "Keep it. You're in charge of communications. Click the link Thalia sends you and you can track their location."

"Got it. They're a good ten minutes away." Gabe was close, his breath fanning the back of her hair. "What do we do? I know you. You're not a sit-and-wait kind of girl."

The window at the back corner of the vehicle shattered as another gunshot rang out.

Gabe ducked, and Hannah flinched and tried to find the shooter's nest.

Somewhere out of sight, a horn beeped, adding urgency to the moment.

The angle of fire had changed. If they stayed where they were, they would quickly run out of time. She could move to the other side of the vehicle, but that would only buy them a few moments. It wouldn't be long before their assailant was close enough to simply circle the SUV and fire at will.

Their only hope was to run for it and find cover in the trees.

Motioning Gabe forward, she inched to the front of the SUV before the rear passenger window rained glass to the gravel. "We're going to make a run for that bend in the road about fifty yards ahead, then we're going to drop down into the ravine and take cover in the trees."

"The trees where the guy with the gun is hiding?" Gabe's voice was level, but tight.

A bullet pinged into the passenger door, punctuating his question.

"Got a better idea?" They had to go now. The way their pursuer was maneuvering, he was seconds from a clear shot. "Get moving."

Urging Gabe ahead of her, Hannah sprinted for

the curve that would offer concealment, if only for a moment.

Why were there no cars coming from the opposite direction? If someone had blocked that part of the road as well, they might have two people gunning for them. They could be pinned in the middle of the shallow woodland that dropped off into a deep ravine.

Cornered.

Even if a car did come, did she dare trust that the occupants weren't going to murder them?

No, concealing themselves in the trees until Thalia and Phillip arrived was the only way to save their lives.

They hit the tree line at full speed, only slowing when Gabe nearly decapitated himself on a low-hanging branch. They were safe for a few seconds. Long enough to catch their breath and to plot a move.

The area would be peaceful under other circumstances. A carpet of pine needles blanketed the dirt around undergrowth that thickened as it neared the edge of the ravine. A creek flowed about thirty feet down at the base of sheer rock. The trees, leafing for spring, offered a cool dampness that comforted Hannah's hot skin.

Hot from exertion, and because she'd lost control again. How many times was this guy going to get the jump on them? How had she missed the signs? Their flat tire was no accident. Somehow, he'd gotten close without Hannah seeing him.

This was her fault.

Gabe leaned against a tree, heaving in air and watching her phone screen. "Thalia and Phillip are stopped about half a mile away."

"So our guy did block the road." It's what she would do, and what she'd suspected all along. "We'll hunker down until they get here." Hiding would be tricky though. The trees were thinner than they were around the curve. They offered better cover than the open roadway, but they were still in spring budding. There weren't enough leaves to offer true concealment.

That could work to their advantage. If the shooter could see them, they could see him.

Hannah glanced around and then pointed to the edge of the ravine. "That underbrush. We'll get into it and stay low. We'll see him before he sees us." *Hopefully.*

Following her lead, Gabe burrowed into the brush ahead of her, finding a space between two large bushes. Thorns and branches tore at Hannah's clothes, scratching her hands, and there was a fine graze running along Gabe's cheek.

Hopefully, that would be the only blood drawn today. Normally, she would be more confident, but this was Gabe. If she let him die on her watch…

That was more than she could bear to think about.

She'd already hurt him once. She couldn't let him endure any more pain because of her.

"It's not your fault." Gabe's low whisper came from her right, where he was flat to the ground among the undergrowth.

Either he could read her thoughts or she'd said that aloud, a definite risk in a moment like this. She ignored him. Talking could get them both killed.

From the left, a twig snapped. The trees fell silent. Birds stopped singing. A few squirrels raced into higher branches and hunkered down.

Hannah held her breath, listening for small sounds over the light breeze in the treetops and the gurgle of the creek far below. A faint rustle on dried leaves revealed slow, methodical footfalls.

Loyal Readers
FREE BOOKS Voucher

We're giving away

THOUSANDS

of

FREE

BOOKS

LOVE INSPIRED
INSPIRATIONAL ROMANCE

Her Secret Son
LINDA GOODNIGHT
NEW YORK TIMES BESTSELLING AUTHOR

She'll do anything for her baby

LARGER PRINT

ROMANCE

LOVE INSPIRED SUSPENSE
INSPIRATIONAL ROMANCE

Rescue Mission
LYNETTE EASON
USA TODAY BESTSELLING AUTHOR

ROCKY MOUNTAIN K-9 UNIT

LARGE PRINT

SUSPENSE

Don't Miss Out! Send for Your Free Books Today!

See Details Inside

Get up to 4
FREE FABULOUS BOOKS
You Love!

To thank you for being a loyal reader we'd like to send you up to 4 FREE BOOKS, absolutely free when you try the Harlequin Reader Service.

Just write "YES" on the Loyal Reader Voucher and we'll send you 2 free books from each series you choose and Free Mystery Gifts, altogether worth over $20.

Try **Love Inspired® Romance Larger-Print** and get 2 books and fall in love with inspirational romances that take you on an uplifting journey of faith, forgiveness and hope.

Try **Love Inspired® Suspense Larger-Print** and get 2 books where courage and optimism unite in stories of faith and love in the face of danger.

Or **TRY BOTH and get 2 books from each series!**

Your free books are completely free, even the shipping! If you continue with your subscription, you can look forward to curated monthly shipments of brand-new books from your selected series, always at a discount off the cover price! Plus you can cancel any time.

So don't miss out, return your Loyal Readers Voucher today to get your Free books.

Pam Powers

LOYAL READER
FREE BOOKS VOUCHER

◄ DETACH AND MAIL CARD TODAY! ▼

© 2022 HARLEQUIN ENTERPRISES ULC
™ and ® are trademarks owned by Harlequin Enterprises ULC. Printed in the U.S.A.

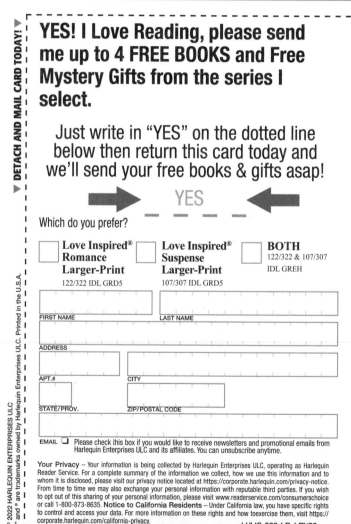

YES! I Love Reading, please send me up to 4 FREE BOOKS and Free Mystery Gifts from the series I select.

Just write in "YES" on the dotted line below then return this card today and we'll send your free books & gifts asap!

➡ YES ⬅

Which do you prefer?

☐ **Love Inspired®**
Romance
Larger-Print
122/322 IDL GRD5

☐ **Love Inspired®**
Suspense
Larger-Print
107/307 IDL GRD5

☐ **BOTH**
122/322 & 107/307
IDL GREH

FIRST NAME

LAST NAME

ADDRESS

APT.#

CITY

STATE/PROV.

ZIP/POSTAL CODE

EMAIL ☐ Please check this box if you would like to receive newsletters and promotional emails from Harlequin Enterprises ULC and its affiliates. You can unsubscribe anytime.

Your Privacy – Your information is being collected by Harlequin Enterprises ULC, operating as Harlequin Reader Service. For a complete summary of the information we collect, how we use this information and to whom it is disclosed, please visit our privacy notice located at https://corporate.harlequin.com/privacy-notice. From time to time we may also exchange your personal information with reputable third parties. If you wish to opt out of this sharing of your personal information, please visit www.readerservice.com/consumerschoice or call 1-800-873-8635. **Notice to California Residents** – Under California law, you have specific rights to control and access your data. For more information on these rights and how to exercise them, visit https://corporate.harlequin.com/california-privacy.

LI/LIS 622 LR LEV22

◆ HARLEQUIN Reader Service — **Here's how it works:**

Accepting your 2 free books and 2 free gifts (gifts valued at approximately $10.00 retail) places you under no obligation to buy anything. You may keep the books and gifts and return the shipping statement marked "cancel." If you do not cancel, approximately one month later we'll send you 6 more books from each series you have chosen, and bill you at our low, subscribers-only discount price. Love Inspired® Romance Larger-Print books and Love Inspired® Suspense Larger-Print books consist of 6 books each month and cost just $6.49 each in the U.S. or $6.74 each in Canada. That is a savings of at least 16% off the cover price. It's quite a bargain! Shipping and handling is just 50¢ per book in the U.S. and $1.25 per book in Canada*. You may return any shipment at our expense and cancel at any time by calling the number below — or you may continue to receive monthly shipments at our low, subscribers-only discount price plus shipping and handling

▲ If offer card is missing write to: Harlequin Reader Service, P.O. Box 1341, Buffalo, NY 14240-8531 or visit www.ReaderService.com ▲

BUSINESS REPLY MAIL
FIRST-CLASS MAIL   PERMIT NO. 717   BUFFALO, NY

POSTAGE WILL BE PAID BY ADDRESSEE

HARLEQUIN READER SERVICE
PO BOX 1341
BUFFALO NY 14240-8571

NO POSTAGE
NECESSARY
IF MAILED
IN THE
UNITED STATES

No shadow approached. Wherever their assailant was, he was close, and he was good at staying hidden.

Hannah tightened her grip on her pistol and dared to slowly look behind her. If they had to run, their only way out was down. The ravine was a straight rock face about six feet behind them. There was nothing to break their fall or to conceal them.

Lord, don't let him spot us.

Beside her, Gabe's breaths slowed until Hannah wasn't even certain he was still breathing. Passing out would be the worst thing he could do, but with the footsteps drawing nearer, she didn't dare elbow him or remind him to inhale.

Closer.

The shadows shifted. If she could trust her senses, the gunman was about five yards away between them and the road. The slow pace said the person was carefully scanning as they walked, tracking their earlier movements. If the shooter drew closer, broken branches would surely give away their hiding spot.

Suddenly, the sounds around them changed. Accelerating car engines raced by on the road, vehicle after vehicle, as traffic began to flow.

The footsteps stopped. Hannah could just make out a figure facing the road, a dark hood covering his head.

Did she dare try to take him into custody? He held answers. If she moved fast enough, she could take him down. But if she moved too slowly, the bullets would fly.

Hers could hit a passing car.

His could hit Gabe.

Hannah's muscles tensed to rise. She'd have to take the chance. On the road, a car raced up, tires squealing as it came to a halt.

"Federal agents!" Thalia's voice rang off the mountain. "Put down your weapon and lace your fingers behind your head!"

Hannah didn't move. If he was a hardened assassin, he'd fire on them and die before he obeyed.

For a moment, no one moved. *Come on. Give up. Don't turn this into—*

With a curse, their pursuer bolted into the trees and ran back toward the curve.

"Seriously?" Phillip's exclamation came from the road.

Thalia ran.

Hannah leaped up, limbs and thorns dragging at her clothing. She aimed in the direction the suspect had fled, but he'd already disappeared.

By the time Hannah freed herself from the underbrush and made sure Gabe was okay, Thalia was back. "I lost him. He either hid like you guys did, took a dive off of the ravine or he made it to safety somehow."

Hannah holstered her pistol and tried to swipe dead leaves and twigs from her jeans and her black fleece jacket. "Did you get a good look at him?"

"Dark hoodie. Jeans. Average height and weight. Nothing good to go on." Thalia stared in the direction their assailant had run. "I don't think he's a pro."

There was no way. A professional hitter wouldn't have spooked. "Phillip?"

"He's up the road, probably seeing if our guy comes out at any point. The guy used his pickup to block the road and then came down here after you. A couple of people got fed up waiting and shoved the truck to the shoulder. I'd be willing to go on record that it's probably stolen."

Most likely. "And traffic from the other direction?"

"It just so happens, there's construction ahead. The road is down to one lane. Your guy was gutsy, chancing your tire would go full flat before you got to where there were more witnesses or that he'd get the job done before they let a line of cars through."

"Gutsy or stupid." Hannah resisted scratching where a branch had whipped against her cheek and turned to Gabe, who had stepped up beside her. "You okay?"

"Probably having a minor heart attack. Otherwise, I'm amazing." His expression was hard as he stared in the direction the shooter had run, his jaw tight. A fine red line ran down his cheek where a branch had scratched him.

They probably both looked a mess.

When his gaze caught hers, there was icy determination in his blue eyes. "We're still going to talk to Trevor."

She wanted to tell him no. That after this, it would be much better if he went into protective custody or, at the very least, hunkered down at home with someone to watch over him.

But she knew that look. Gabe was determined. He'd threatened last night to go without her, and she didn't dare challenge that determination.

There might be a lot of things spinning out of control in her life, but she wouldn't let Gabe be one of them. As long as she kept him in sight, she had a fighting chance of keeping him alive. Vigilance was needed now more than ever, and she wouldn't trust him to another agent.

She would keep him safe, even if it meant giving up everything.

Gabe drummed his fingers on a metal table in a visitation room, staring at the door where Trevor would enter. While the scratch on his cheek itched like wild-fire, he resisted the urge to touch it. The last thing he wanted was to appear nervous when Trevor walked in. He squared his shoulders and tried to relax, but he'd never visited anyone in prison before.

This was nothing like TV.

It was chilly in the stark room that housed only a table and chairs bolted to the floor. Because Trevor wasn't a violent offender, he'd be handcuffed but not shackled.

It was disconcerting to know he was about to face the man who'd been his best friend and roommate for years. The truth was, there was a measure of fear in his heart, especially since he'd had no contact with Trevor since the arrest.

Guilt had kept him away. Trevor had caused his own problems, but Gabe had never come to grips with being the one to turn him in. He'd chosen to stay away, as had Hannah.

It felt odd that this Hannah had dated Trevor. How did she feel having dated a convicted felon?

It was hard to tell. She sat beside Gabe, flipping through a folder containing records of Trevor's phone calls and visitors. She'd said little on the remainder of the drive, constantly checking the rearview mirror to make sure Thalia and Phillip were behind them.

Since they'd entered the small room with the guard posted outside, Hannah had been focused and silent, seemingly absorbed with the pages before her.

Either the shooter or Trevor's impending entrance had rattled her.

Gabe wouldn't lie. The gunfire had shaken him. The attack had shown him how helpless he was in a face-to-face fight. It was one thing to battle the corporate world's bullies from behind a screen by preemptively identifying them before they could step into a position of power, but there were worse bullies in the world. Assassins who killed. Terrorists who destroyed.

If someone had flagged the guy who'd fired at them today sooner, maybe they wouldn't have been on the receiving end of those bullets. It was possible Hannah was right, and his talents could be better used chasing—

The metal door opened, and a guard ushered Trevor in.

Reflexively, Gabe stood. Although Trevor was a couple of inches taller, Gabe felt better facing him on his feet.

Trevor's gaze immediately locked on to Gabe, his eyes widening. Sliding into the chair across the table, he rested his cuffed hands in front of him and stared as though he couldn't believe it. "Gabe?"

Had no one told him who was waiting to see him?

Guilt and fear coursed through Gabe as he sat, though his rational mind said he shouldn't feel either. He'd done the right thing turning Trevor in, and Trevor had never been violent or angry. Prison could change a man though.

Trevor shook his head and sat back. "It's been a while." His tone was unreadable. "I got arrested, and you disappeared. Couldn't even bother to stand by my side." He sniffed, and his passive expression shifted into a sneer. "I guess that's what happens when you turn your buddy over to the FBI, huh? You run? That how you got those scratches on your face? Still running?"

Under the table, Gabe balled his fists. Trevor was purposely poking at Gabe's weakness. He knew Gabe's past, knew how he'd often hid from the bullies who'd tormented him, and now he was using that knowledge to inflict pain.

Trevor's sneer faded when Gabe didn't react. "What are you doing here anyway? Why now? I was told a federal agent wanted to talk to me about a hack and identity theft. But it couldn't be me." For the first time, his gaze flicked to Hannah. "I have no access..."

As Trevor leaned across the table to get a closer look at her face, Hannah shut the folder, laced her fingers on top of it and stared into his eyes, unflinching.

Trevor's eyes narrowed. "Hannah?" He glanced between the two of them and then made a deliberate show of looking at her hands. "You two hook up or get married or something after I got put away?" The edge in his voice said he was trying to sound angry, but pain overlaid the words. "Is this why I never heard from either of you?"

"No." Hannah's voice was brusque and business-like. She pulled her credentials from her hip pocket and showed them to Trevor. "Chief Warrant Officer Hannah Austin. I'm an investigator with the United States Army. I have questions, but you are free not to answer and to return to your cell at any time." She pulled a photo and one of the visitor log sheets from the file and slid it across the table to Trevor. "About five weeks ago, a woman came to visit you. Sadie Lawson. Do you remember her?"

"You're an investigator?" Trevor looked at Gabe. The man wasn't angry like Gabe had expected. He seemed confused. "Makes sense. Weren't you studying criminal justice at Brevard or something? Back when we were *dating*?" He hit the word hard, almost as though he was accusing her of something.

"Sadie Lawson?" Hannah tapped the photo, not taking his bait. "You spoke to her?"

The questions seemed to throw Trevor off-balance. He shook his head like a dog flinging off water. "Yeah. Sadie came here."

"Why?"

"No idea. I'd never heard of her before she showed up. And..." Trevor shifted, waving his cuffed hands between Hannah and Gabe. "I need a second. What's going on? I was told that a federal investigator wanted to speak to me." He stared at Hannah. "You're the federal agent?"

"I already told you that." Hannah's voice softened. She was likely as surprised by Trevor's demeanor as Gabe was. The anger they'd anticipated simply wasn't there. She pulled the photo and log sheet toward her and slipped them into the folder. "What did Sadie want, Trevor?"

"Are you two dating?"

"No." Gabe answered before Hannah could. This was going on too long. The guilt of not only calling the FBI but also of not reaching out to Trevor sooner was gnawing holes in his stomach. He regretted that earlier cup of coffee. Regretted not being a friend when Trevor had needed one.

Looking at him now was harder than Gabe had imagined. It looped the past onto the present. Trevor's hair was shorter, and his prison jumpsuit was a far cry from his designer clothes in college, but he was still Trevor. The guy Gabe had played pickup basketball with. Who'd befriended Gabe when he'd felt like the bullied nerd. Who'd helped Gabe study for calculus tests even though he hated the subject.

Then again, Trevor was also the guy who'd stolen

Hannah out from under him and had always seemed to make him feel slightly smaller, not only in stature but in social rank.

Still…

"I should have come to see you sooner." The words were out before Gabe considered them.

Beside him, Hannah stiffened but remained silent.

Trevor exhaled slowly. "Yeah, you should have."

Hannah knocked her knuckles on the table, drawing their attention. "I'm sorry to break this up."

This wasn't a social call. This was life or death.

"Trevor, what did Sadie want?" The words were firm. There would be no more stalling.

Dragging his hand down his face, Trevor looked at Hannah, accepting defeat. "She said she had proof that Gabe was the one who'd called the FBI and that he'd used some illegal program on my laptop. He'd violated my privacy. I don't really know all the details."

The roiling in Gabe's stomach turned into a full-blown tsunami. Shoving away from the table, he walked over to stand by the hall door and stare through the wire-laced window.

His role in the case was supposed to be confidential. No one knew. How had Sadie Lawson found out?

Behind him, Hannah spoke. "FBI informants are classified information. It's likely Sadie broke the law."

"I have no idea. Look." Trevor's jumpsuit rustled, and the sound was too loud in the room. "This woman I've never seen before shows up here. She says she works for this New Justice Network and she can get me out on a technicality. I really don't care what the technicality is. If she can get me out, I want out. If she can wipe the slate clean, I want that too. She says all I have to do is cooperate."

"But you were guilty."

"I said there was enough evidence to prove I was guilty. I never admitted anything. I couldn't..." The silence dragged on until Gabe faced the table again. Trevor was staring at the ceiling. "I couldn't drag my parents through a trial, so I did what I could to keep from hurting them more."

"Admirable." Hannah flipped open the folder again. It was tough to tell if she meant the statement or if she was being sarcastic. "What does Sadie want you to 'cooperate' with?"

"Just to let NJN fight on my behalf. Accept any interviews she sends my way. Use the talking points she gives me." He shrugged. "That's it."

Hannah made a few notes in her phone and then tapped her finger against the side of the device. "Sadie pursued you?"

"Yes." Trevor sounded as though he was as lost as Gabe felt.

"Do you have access to any technology?"

Trevor laughed so sharply that the sound echoed off the walls like a gunshot. "No. I'm in here for hacking and extortion. They're not about to let me touch anything that isn't on a closed system. Why?" He glanced at Gabe and back to Hannah. "Look, if there's hacking going on, it's not me. I just want out of here." He suddenly looked younger than his thirty-odd years. His voice dropped. "I'm in here with guys who ran international drug cartels. This is..." He swallowed hard. "I just want out."

Hannah appeared unmoved by Trevor's emotion. "Is there anything else you can tell us about Sadie?"

He sighed with resignation and slumped in his chair. "That's pretty much it. And before you ask, I've had no correspondence, no letters, nothing from her since that day. I signed paperwork agreeing to let NJN fight for me. That's it."

"And she wants nothing in return?"

"Nothing." He looked up at Gabe. "Sadie said, if I get out because of whatever program you used, I have the right to sue you for the profits. Is that true?"

"Profits?" There was only one copy, and it was hidden. Sadie Lawson shouldn't know a thing about it. Unleashing software that was a legal and ethical nightmare was unthinkable.

Hannah smiled slightly, but Gabe had no idea why. "Thank you, Trevor." She shut the folder and moved to stand.

"Wait." Gabe stepped closer to the table. "You're not angry at me?" It seemed unfathomable that Trevor could know the truth about Gabe turning him in and not be furious.

"I was, but the prosecutors told me I was a suspect before someone informed on me. They had an undercover agent already working my case. All you did was speed up the process." Trevor stood, and the guard behind him stepped closer. "But hear me on this, Gabe. Sadie is very interested in money, and she'll do whatever it takes to get what's owed to me…and to her. Believe me, all that she's done so far? She's capable of far worse."

TEN

"So Sadie Lawson is using Trevor Haskell." In the parking lot, Phillip leaned against Hannah's SUV and stared at the front of the prison. Bright sunlight reflected off the windshield, making it hard to look directly at him. "Why?"

Hannah looked away and scanned the area. They'd parked far enough from other cars so that they could talk freely, but she still wanted to make sure no one was listening. It was likely safer to confer here than at Gabe's. There was no way to know for sure if his house had been bugged.

She'd have Thalia do a sweep when they got back. For now, they needed to sort out the truckload of information that Trevor had dumped on them.

Gabe squinted against the sunlight. There was no shade in the prison parking lot. "Once again, someone brought up my software."

"Let's start there." Thalia was sitting on the hood of her car with her hands braced on either side of her hips, watching Gabe. "What's the deal with this program?"

Gabe looked to Hannah as though waiting for her to respond, but the story was his to tell. When it was clear she wasn't going to talk, he stepped closer to the three agents. "The short version?"

Phillip looked up from tugging at something on the sleeve of his jacket. "Unless you're offering popcorn, let's keep it under a minute. We missed lunch."

It looked like Gabe almost smiled, but it might have been a trick of the midday sunlight. "Short version is that I profile people based on their behavior in real life, but I also analyze online behavior. With my grad school mentor, I developed a program that would do the online work for me. Feed it their social media, their online purchases, their browser history and other bits of data. It builds a profile that can then be melded with in-person evals, if there are any. It has the ability to remote into a computer as well, so if you had a warrant and couldn't get physical hands on a person's phone or laptop, then—"

"Then your program could hack in and mine the necessary data." Thalia leaned forward, clearly intrigued.

"And that's how my software discovered that Trevor was blackmailing a senator."

The pain in Gabe's expression was so raw, Hannah wanted to close the couple of feet between them and take his hand. Seeing Trevor hadn't been easy for him. It had to have reopened wounds. Realizing that Trevor knew his role was something Gabe would have to process and work through.

Both men seemed to know everything except Hannah's past role as an undercover agent. That would have to remain a secret, particularly now that NJN had taken on Trevor's case.

She forced herself to look away from Gabe. Once he found out she'd used him back then...

"It takes a lot of fortitude to turn your best friend

over to the FBI. That wasn't easy." Phillip broke the silence. There was new respect in his gaze as he tipped his head toward Gabe.

Gabe looked away.

"But this program..." Phillip was warming up to the topic. As the technical expert to Thalia's muscle, he'd naturally be interested in that part of the story. "Sounds like it would be a boon to investigations."

"More like a serious violation of the constitutional right to privacy." Gabe shoved his hands into his pockets and watched as a car passed them on its way off the property. He waited for it to exit the lot before he spoke. "Dr. Mathison and I realized it would be easy to weaponize the software, to turn it into a spider that crawled around the web and looked for vulnerabilities. It could profile anyone from anywhere, without their knowledge. Not only that, but in the hands of a foreign government, a terror cell or organized crime, it could easily start pinging fake identities."

"Gotcha." Thalia was all in now too. "What you're saying is, we wouldn't have to worry about bad actors getting lists of undercover agents or protected witnesses. They could just deploy the software and wait."

"Exactly. The program would sniff them out with a high degree of accuracy." Gabe glanced at Hannah as though she could give him the strength to keep talking. "I destroyed all but one copy, which I have hidden off-line and heavily encrypted."

Hannah stepped into the center of the three of them, anxious to move the conversation forward. She felt exposed in the parking lot. "Why keep a copy?" It had nagged at her since the first time he'd mentioned it.

"Sentimentality?" Gabe shrugged. "Dr. M and I

worked on it together. He had cancer. Mentoring me was basically a labor of love. He agreed that I should shelve it, but I couldn't bring myself to destroy it. Now though? I think the sooner it's gone, the better."

That was debatable. In the right hands, Gabe's work could save lives.

"If he's dead, who else would know about it? Did you keep notes?" Thalia asked. "This has come up more than once, so this isn't someone guessing. They *know*."

"All of my notes were kept in a handwritten journal to avoid hacks. I shredded and burned it years ago."

"And Dr. Mathison?" Gabe's former mentor could be the weak link, even though he was gone.

"He didn't have anything. I kept all the copies of notes. We worked solely on my laptop and avoided any sort of crossover between machines. He'd worked with a colleague who was accused of plagiarizing a mentee's work, so he made sure there was never any way someone could say he'd done the same."

"Maybe he talked about it to his wife?" Phillip glanced at his watch, probably thinking it was past time to get this show on the road and into a drive-thru.

Hannah was feeling pretty depleted herself. Sweet tea and a chicken sandwich wouldn't hurt. But Phillip might be on to something. "Gabe, have you talked to Mrs. Mathison since this started?"

"Briefly, and only in generalities."

There may be answers there. "Give her a call. Ask if she remembers anything Dr. Mathison said about your work together, but don't mention the program. Maybe he let something slip. Does anyone else live in their house? Other family? Anyone who could have overheard a conversation or seen an email?"

"We didn't email about the program or Trevor. They

only had a son, a year or so younger than me. He moved out before I met them. They didn't talk about him much, but I always thought they were so good to me because they missed him."

"Not a replacement for their son, but someone who helped fill the void?" She could appreciate that. A teacher in middle school had noticed Hannah's pain over her family situation. She'd been a good listener and had soothed some of the ache in Hannah's soul. "Have you memorized Mrs. Mathison's number?"

Gabe nodded.

She passed him her cell phone. "Call her."

He hesitated, then took the phone and walked a few feet away to make the call.

Phillip watched. "Should we be listening?"

"No." Hannah watched Gabe's back as he talked, his voice a low rumble that floated toward them on the warm spring breeze. "I doubt we get anything from this, though I may want to talk to her later based on what she says to Gabe. I highly doubt she's a suspect. She could have simply asked Gabe about the app. It would make no sense for her to hire assassins." She shook her head, picturing Sadie Lawson and her onstage swagger. "My gut says someone at NJN is behind all of this."

"My gut's with you." Thalia hopped off her car and dug into her pocket for the keys. "NJN takes in too much money. We peeked at the online component of that little silent auction the other night, and the take was high. Higher than you'd think for a start-up justice advocacy group. They know the right donors to pitch to and the right cases to pull in."

"Trevor Haskell is high profile." Phillip knocked his fist lightly against the SUV door and studied the sky as though he was searching for memories. "His case was all over the news because it was pretty salacious. A grad student infiltrating the senate and trying to sway policy just for the thrill of it? People still talk about it. There have been a few documentaries, some podcasts. NJN is the first to assert his innocence though. It won't take much for this to make national news and to shove NJN into the spotlight. That opens the door to a lot more fundraising opportunities."

It all came back to the money. Every time. "You know, Trevor said something interesting. He said Sadie told him he could sue Gabe for the software and sell it. I'm guessing NJN would want a cut of the profits."

Phillip whistled low. "With the right buyer, a program like that could go for some really big money. *Really* big. And if someone licensed it to agencies and corporations instead of selling it outright? That could mean revenue for decades."

Gabe ended his call and came back, passing the phone to Hannah. "Nothing. She didn't mention Trevor either, so I doubt Dr. M told her I was involved in that."

So if the intel source wasn't Jeanette Mathison, who was it? Hannah tapped her index fingers against her lower lip. They needed to get to the basement level, the very bottom, the first mention of the program to Gabe.

And that wasn't Sadie Lawson.

It was Gabe's boss, Leigh Lewis.

Leigh Lewis of Skylark Profiling, whose employee, Quentin Fisher, had been at the NJN fundraiser. Hannah straightened. "Have we heard back from Dana with the background check on Quentin Fisher?"

Phillip nodded. "Dana talked to us before we headed back. The guy's squeaky clean."

"Gabe?" Hannah started to ask if he'd be willing to use his program to check out Quentin. Something in her gut told her it was a thread to follow. Something else in her gut said Gabe would never go for it.

She changed tactics, and he waited for her to speak again. "You're not banned from entering your office, are you? There's nothing that's happened on that front that you haven't told me?" Unless he had some sort of legal order against him, as co-owner, he had every right to walk into that building and access the system or read up on his employees.

"No." He narrowed his eyes. "Why?"

"Do you have access to employee files on the closed network?"

"I do. My log-ins are still intact. The data breach didn't reach them."

Perfect. "What do you say we go tonight and do some fishing? I want to see if we can find anything in the system that would indicate Leigh Lewis or Quentin Fisher are involved in this."

Gabe froze, and Hannah half expected an argument, but then he simply nodded. "Okay."

"It's going to require you to play field agent. I'd prefer no one find out you were there."

This time, he really did smile. "If it will end this, I'll do whatever it takes."

Hannah bit the tip of her tongue. That's what she was most afraid of.

"You know the instant I key into the building, I make myself visible." Gabe stood at the back entrance to Skylark Profiling, employee card poised near the entry lock. One swipe of his card and four punches to the keypad, and he'd be in. "If anyone is watching the security feed or the entry logs, they'll know immediately."

"That's why we're here." Hannah's voice in his earpiece calmed his nerves a bit, but it didn't change the facts. Going into Skylark alone at night while an assassin was on the loose made him a proverbial sitting duck. "You're not alone."

How had she known what he was thinking? "Feels like it," he muttered. He was the only one standing at the door. The only one entering the building.

Hannah had wanted plausible deniability in order to protect him. If he went in by himself, he could say he wanted to catch up on the work he'd missed over the past two days or that he'd left something behind. If Hannah or anyone else from Overwatch entered with him, all of that went away. Leigh and Quentin would know they were looking into Skylark, and if either of them had anything to do with the attacks...

They could all be dead before the sun rose.

"I'm right here, Gabe." There was Hannah's voice again, inside his head. Sort of the same way she'd managed to ease back inside his heart.

But he wasn't thinking about that right now. Not at all.

"Thalia and Phillip are stationed around the building. I'm right across the street. If anything goes down, we've got you. I promise."

It was that promise that got him sliding his card through the lock and keying in his passcode.

The door clicked, and he stepped into the cool hallway. It was lit only by dim overnight lights at intervals that left puddles of darkness on the floor. "I'm in."

He winced. That sounded so dramatic, like he'd picked a lock or blown the door open with whatever explosives action-movie heroes used.

Really, what had he done? Unlocked a door. He was a

downright rock star. He could almost hear Thalia laughing at his unintentional theatrics.

"You've got this." Hannah's voice through his earpiece seemed to permeate his entire being in the best of ways. "Pretend it's a normal workday. Walk up the hall, go in your office and run a background check."

"And hook up the external drive to my computer." The drive that was practically burning a hole in his back pocket was one of Phillip's babies. Logging into the system gave Gabe access. Hooking up Phillip's toy gave Phillip entrée to Skylark's closed system through Gabe's log-in. He could download or crawl through files at will.

As co-owner, Gabe had given him permission, so there was no need for a warrant. "You know I own half of the company. We could have just walked right in and done what we wanted."

"This way doesn't tip our hand. You belong here. We don't. And Phillip's program won't leave a trace on the system, so no one will know. We're not looking at employee records specifically. We're searching for emails, texts, anything that would indicate someone inside Skylark has had contact with Sadie Lawson."

Or that someone wanted Gabe to suffer and die.

He shuddered.

At his office door, he glanced around as though he was the one doing something wrong, then he swiped in. "Is Phillip ready? I'm in the office. I'll be logged on within the next two minutes."

He kept the lights off. Swiping his mouse lit up all four screens, and the Skylark logo flashed to life and asked for his passcode. He typed it in then, and as the machine booted, he slipped the drive from his pocket and plugged it in. Clicking to the file system, he opened the hard drive and started the program. "It's done."

It sounded like he'd assassinated someone.

Hmm. That might hit a little too close to home.

Gabe tapped his fingers lightly against the keyboard as Phillip went to work in the background. He had no doubt that Hannah's shadow investigators had run their own checks on everyone they suspected, from Sadie Lawson to Leigh Lewis to Quentin Fisher. He also had no doubt that they employed some high-level profilers.

But he wanted to know for himself. Did he dare build a profile on Leigh and Quentin? He couldn't legally search up Sadie, but Leigh and Quentin worked with and for him. As employees of Skylark, they'd all given permission for random searches as needed.

He tipped his head and stared at the ceiling. There was no experimental software involved, but this was starting to feel entirely too much like what had happened with Trevor.

Someone he trusted could be a criminal. They could land in prison.

Because of him.

He swallowed the guilt. No matter what happened next, this had to stop. It was in his power to *make* it stop. What Hannah and her team did was important. Was he meant to do this as well?

Would it impress Hannah if he did? Show her he was the kind of man she deserved?

He shook his head. This moment required focus. "I can work while you do your thing, right, Phillip?" He spoke low, knowing the jaw mic would pick up the question.

"Sure thing."

"What are you thinking?" That was Hannah's voice, and it was etched with something he couldn't read.

"I'm thinking of building a profile on Leigh and Quentin," he muttered, already pulling up Quentin's employee records to get his birthdate and his social to use in a search. "I might be able to find—"

The room plunged into darkness as the computer monitors went black. The hum of machines fell silent. The hall lights died, and the emergency lights over the exits clicked on with a feeble glow.

"What just happened?" Phillip's voice was level but urgent, as though he didn't want to induce panic, but he was already on the move.

"Power's gone."

"Get out of there. Now." Hannah's order held an urgency that Phillip's hadn't. It was a lot less professional. It bordered on panic.

He didn't want to read into that.

Instead, Gabe reached for the cable that connected Phillip's drive to the computer and eyed the door. It was a straight shot to—

The front window shattered, and something smacked into the far wall.

Gabe dropped to the floor and backed up against the side of his desk, his heart in his throat. He scanned the room in the dim light. A divot marred the wall opposite the window. There was a good chance that had he not stepped away from his desk when he had, that bullet might have been lodged in him.

"Gabe?" Hannah again. "Answer me." Her words were clipped, as though she was running.

"I'm fine." *No. Not fine. Numb.*

"Get somewhere you can take cover. A bathroom.

Somewhere small and concealed. We're circling the building, trying to cut off the shooter."

This was middle school again. The taunts had grown fierce. The fists had flown. Back then, he'd stepped outside himself into a zone where reality was three steps behind him. It had been the only way to survive.

He was there now. Distanced from events around him.

He had to survive.

The boy he used to be wanted to obey Hannah's orders and hide in the bathroom, curled up in the fetal position. But this wasn't middle school. As anger at the present and how he'd been beaten in the past rose, the man he was now wanted to leap out the window and rip the gun from his assailant's hand.

But he wasn't the only person in play. If he went rogue, he could get Hannah and the others killed.

That was something he could never live with.

He'd fight whatever fight came to him. And that started with his computer. "Phillip, did you get what you needed?"

"I got something. Close to enough."

"I'm retrieving the drive." He had to get to it before whoever fired that shot either made a full-frontal assault or started peppering the room from a distance. The shooter had to assume they'd either hit Gabe or he'd evacuated, but if they wanted him dead, they'd also want to see proof.

"Gabe." Hannah's voice was a warning, an order and a cry of fear, rolled into one.

He ignored it. Crouching, he slipped around the corner of the desk. The design of the furniture left him no cover. Tensing against a bullet that might come next, he crouched and grabbed the cable. Pulling it free, he shoved the drive into his pocket and ran for the door, hunched below window level.

In the doorway, he hesitated, listening, afraid to ask for a status update because someone might hear him, though they clearly already knew he was in his office.

The building was silent. As his ears tuned in, the quiet, familiar sounds began to emerge. The distant hum of the backup generator that powered their servers. The whirr of fans from the server room around the corner.

The server room. Only three people had a key, Quentin, Leigh and himself. It was reinforced with a steel door and a double lock to deter thieves looking for a quick buck. That was his place of refuge.

He just prayed no one had slipped into the building and was creeping toward him.

In the windowless hallway, he dared to stand. Pressing his back to the wall, he eased toward the corner, trying to keep his heart rate and his breathing paced.

"Gabe, you good? Yes or no is all I need." Hannah would worry if he didn't answer quickly.

"Yes." He hoped she heard that whisper.

At the corner, he stopped. Up the hallway, a door eased shut with a soft click. It sounded like the heavy fire door that divided the main lobby from the offices. It stayed locked, accessible only by key card.

Whoever was coming either had access or had stolen access, and they now had a direct line of sight to the server-room door.

They were also heading toward him.

Curiosity wanted him to peek, to see if he recognized his would-be killer. But with no cover, his *would-be* killer would become his *actual* murderer.

Gabe pressed closer to the wall and eased back toward his office.

From around the corner, light footsteps fell softly in the stillness. The door to the server room jiggled.

They were close. The hall to the back door was too long to run. He'd be caught dead to rights in a gunman's sights if he tried. The sound of his footfalls would give him away before he could get to the exit. Even then, the parking lot was wide open until he reached his vehicle.

His only cover was in his office, but that would be the next place the gunman headed.

There was nowhere to hide. He had to make a stand. And he had about ten seconds to figure out how.

He slipped into his office, searching the semidarkness for anything to use as a weapon. His diplomas were framed on a wall in the corner. He'd had them professionally done. Heavy wood. Thick glass.

He slipped his MIT sheepskin off the wall and stood by the door where he wouldn't be spotted through the windows that faced the hall. He held the frame over his head as the shuffle of footsteps drew closer.

A soft shadow fell across the doorway, barely illuminated by the emergency lights in the hall.

Gabe held his breath.

Someone stopped outside the door, listening. They entered the room slowly, pistol leading the way.

When he had a clear shot at the gunman's arm, Gabe swung the diploma frame toward the floor with all his might.

The pistol fired.

ELEVEN

Gabe!

The second gunshot cracked as Hannah reached Gabe's office with Thalia close on her heels. Without key cards and codes, his bullet-shattered window was their only way in.

The sounds of a struggle came from the other side of metal vertical blinds that swayed in the breeze. She ran her gun barrel along the waist-high bottom sill to clear away as many glass shards as possible and then dove inside.

In the shadowy room, two men fought near the door. Hannah took aim as Thalia came through the window behind her. "Federal agents!"

The man closest to the door froze and stepped into the slightly brighter light of the hallway. He wore a mask over the lower half of his face, a bulky dark sweatshirt and blue jeans.

Definitely not Gabe.

He shoved Gabe toward Hannah and ran.

Gabe stumbled backward, righted himself and took off in pursuit.

Had he lost his mind? Their mystery man could fire at any time.

"Gabe! Let us handle it!" She was two steps behind him, running up the hall. If that guy turned, she had no clear shot with Gabe in the way. If he didn't back down, they could all be dead.

Thalia stopped behind her. "I'm going around front." From the sound of her footsteps, she was heading out back to circle the building.

The gunman shoved through the heavy metal doors at the end of the hallway with Gabe close behind. As Gabe rushed to follow, Hannah lowered her pistol, reached out with her free hand and grabbed his shirt, pulling him backward.

He stumbled and nearly fell. Whirling on her, he shoved his hand through his hair. "What are you doing?" He turned as if he was going to charge the door again.

She grabbed his arm. "Wait." When he pulled against her grip, she yelled louder, "Stop!"

The tone of her shout finally got his attention. He stood with his back to her, staring at the door, his shoulders rising and falling as he breathed heavily. "He'll get away."

His voice was so harsh, Hannah dropped his arm and took a step back. Never had she heard him speak with that sort of anger. She bit her lip and eyed him as he glared at her.

No one got to speak to her like that, especially when she'd just stopped them from rushing headlong toward death. When she found her voice, she kept it low and even. "He could have been on the other side of that door, taking aim at whoever blows through it next. He'd have had three bullets in your center mass and been gone before you hit the ground." She shoved down what the image of a bloodied Gabe did to her emotions and focused on him. "I'm going to chalk your tone up to an adrenaline rush."

"My tone?" His face was chiseled stone, and anger flashed in his blue eyes.

"Your tone. You don't talk to me that way." When he moved to speak again, she held up her hand and stepped closer. He needed to understand that he'd nearly gotten himself killed. "Also? You do not disobey me when I tell you what to do. You were directly ordered to shelter in the bathroom, not to go back to your office. Not to—"

"I am *not* one of your soldiers." Gabe bit the words off as though they were ice. "Before you start handing out lectures to me or to anyone else, you need to watch your own *tone.*"

Her eyebrow shot so high that her forehead ached. "Do you not understand that you could have died tonight? All because you decided to be a hero? Now was not the time to show your strength. It was the time to listen. I may not be your commanding officer, but I am in charge here, whether you like it or not."

For a long moment, he stared at her, then he stood taller as though he was forming a way to say the words building in his chest.

She had a feeling she didn't want to hear them.

With a shake of his head, he pulled the external drive from his back pocket, handed it to her and then strode up the hall and around the corner.

His voice buzzed in her earpiece. "Phillip, is it safe to come out?"

"Seems to be. Want me to meet you at the car?"

"Yes."

The back door to the building slammed. A short beep indicated he'd removed his earpiece, probably passing it off to Phillip.

Hannah closed her fingers tighter around the external drive that Gabe had risked his life to save. Her skin burned. With their earpieces in, Phillip and Thalia had heard that entire exchange.

From somewhere in the office complex where Gabe's company was located, sirens approached. Either their presence or the gunshot had tripped an alarm.

She swallowed. "Phillip, Gabe can't leave. He needs to be here when local law enforcement arrives so he can give them his story and vouch for our presence."

"Copy." Phillip's voice was curt. He likely didn't approve of the way she'd spoken to Gabe. He wouldn't ream her out about it, but Thalia would.

Hannah stiffened her spine. She'd say it all again if she had to. Anger laced with fear still coursed hot beneath her skin. They all needed to understand that listening to her and obeying was imperative if they wanted to survive.

Thalia walked around the corner, holstering her pistol as she drew closer and pinning Hannah with her gaze. "You were wrong."

Even though she'd known this was coming, Hannah wasn't in the mood. "I'm going to ignore that. How did you get back in the building?"

Jerking her chin to indicate something behind her, Thalia said, "I came in the same window we came in through the first time. And deflecting with questions doesn't make what you said to Gabe any less wrong."

Normally, she admired Thalia's frank observations, but now was not the time. "All of you need to understand something. I know what I'm talking about. I've been through this before. I know what needs to be done if Gabe wants to survive. If *all of us* want to survive."

Pursing her lips, Thalia shook her head. "Mmm…no."

She held up a finger when Hannah started to argue. "We're the same rank, so you don't get to boss me around quite as much as you think. And Gabe? He's of no rank at all, so you don't get to boss him around for even one second."

Hannah's anger flared hotter. "You, me, Phillip? We're trained agents. We know how this works, what danger looks like. We don't go blasting through doors full tilt and getting ourselves shot. Gabe is a desk jockey. He has no idea how to—"

"You'd better be glad he took out his earpiece, because that was insulting." As the sirens grew louder, filling the hallway with piercing wails, Thalia stepped closer and lowered her voice. "He's a *desk jockey* you wanted on your team. One you supposedly respect. None of this sounds like respect."

As tires screeched to a halt outside the building, Thalia shook her head in disgust and then turned and walked away.

Three o'clock in the morning.

Gabe rolled onto his back and stared at the dark ceiling. Living halfway up a mountain and situated among trees meant the house was dark and quiet, so sleep was almost always restful.

That was not the case tonight.

He kicked off the covers and sat on the edge of the bed, scrubbing his hands down the roughness of his cheeks. He could blame sleeplessness on adrenaline from being shot at, but that would be a lie.

Hannah thought he was weak.

That first moment, when she'd turned on him with fire in her eyes and anger in her voice, he'd bucked. No one had spoken to him that way since high school, not since Dylan Easley had talked down to him in a PE class weeks before graduation. He'd screamed at Gabe across the field. Had called Gabe a loser because he'd missed an easy catch in a pointless, gym-class baseball game.

Of all the taunts he'd endured over the years, that one might have been the worst, because the fallout was brutal. The entire class had joined in the laughter, even his science partner, Trish Anthony, who'd agreed to go to the prom with him. She'd backed out that afternoon.

Gabe stood and paced to the door. There was zero sense in reliving that time in his life. It only dragged him backward.

Most days, he'd overcome the anxiety and the crushed self-esteem. He knew who God said he was, that he was loved and had value. In the eternal sense of things, he rarely had doubts.

But in the earthly sense?

Hannah had wanted him to hide. To cower. To let someone else protect him because she didn't believe he could protect himself. She didn't believe he added value to her team. All that talk about wanting him to work with her had been a lie. In her eyes, he should take cover and wait for rescue.

To Hannah, he was a *desk jockey*. She'd said the words as he'd slipped the earpiece back in when he'd recognized the sound of approaching sirens. The derision in her voice had shriveled his heart. The reproof Thalia had dished out on his behalf had done nothing to make him feel better.

He stepped closer to the door, listening to the silent house, considering another quick workout before deciding against it. He'd already spent an hour in the basement gym, shedding excess energy from his near-death experience and a tense conversation with Leigh when she'd arrived on the scene. She couldn't question his presence since he was co-owner of the company, but it was obvious she was angry and confused.

He'd dodged her queries and her phone calls. There was nothing left to say, not as long as she was a suspect.

Everyone he knew was a suspect.

Gabe leaned forward, hoping to loosen the knot in his stomach. Maybe he'd sit outside. There was peace in his mountainside yard. Peace he desperately needed. He tugged on a sweatshirt and eased the door open.

The house was still. The door to the guest room that Hannah and Thalia were sharing was closed, and the lights were off. Thin blue light filtered under the office door where Phillip was combing through the data they'd mined at the office. Later, he'd hand it over to Gabe.

The thought of profiling his coworkers made him shudder.

He let Phillip know that it was only him moving around the house, then headed out the back door.

The sounds of night were muted by the breeze tossing the trees. Between the newly budding branches, the stars shone bright, broken only by the dark shadow of the mountain rising beyond the meadow.

Settling on the porch swing that sat away from the house at the back of the property, Gabe shoved lightly to start a gentle sway. The chains creaked in the silent night. During the day, the view would stretch across a small meadow burrowed into the mountain that his house stood on. The mountain rising beyond blocked his view of the valley rolling into the distance, but the obstruction was worth it to watch the leaves change with the seasons.

"Mind if I sit here?" The voice from behind made him jump, but he didn't turn. The burn of Hannah's words still lingered. It might not soothe until she was out of his life once more.

But did he really want that?

"Gabe?"

Oh yeah. He should answer. "I don't care." He didn't want to tell her no, but he couldn't bring himself to say yes either. Despite the emotional bruises, there was no turning down a chance to sit beside her.

He couldn't be more double-minded if he tried.

Hannah sat on the edge of the swing and stopped its movement before she slid back and lifted her feet, letting it sway again.

For a long time, she said nothing. She didn't even look at him. Instead, she was absorbed with the heavy chain that held the swing suspended from a thick crossbeam. Her finger trailed the oval of each link.

The silence was too much. It stretched so thin Gabe had to break it. "What made you come out here? There's nothing—"

"You."

The frank word planted his foot, and the swing jerked to a stop. *You.* As though she'd been thinking about him. Wanted to be with him.

Which made no sense, especially given the way she'd talked to and about him.

There was no good response either. "What about me?" sounded silly, like they were in the middle school cafeteria.

He'd hated middle school.

Gabe set the swing in motion again.

Just when he was about to break the silence, she pulled up both feet and crossed her legs on the swing. "I guess I was waiting for you to come out of your room." For a moment, he thought that was all she was going to say, but then she rested her hands on her ankles. "Thalia says I was wrong."

"Thalia was right." He ought to say he'd heard, but that seemed petty. She was smart enough to figure it out.

Her head jerked back. "That was blunt."

He offered a half shrug. Part of him wanted to let her get on with what she needed to say, but the rest of him didn't want this to be easy. His wounds burned with shame and anger that made him want to bite back.

But using words as weapons had built this wall between them. He wouldn't fight back with the very thing he hated.

If only he knew what to say. He wasn't going to apologize. He'd done nothing wrong, and apologizing was something he'd done too often in the past. It had taken years to get over the automatic *sorry* he'd once used to excuse his existence.

Finally, she offered him a slight smile. "I'm used to Thalia being blunt, but you're usually nicer than that."

"You mean *weaker* than that." He winced, gripping the swing between them. His pinky brushed the soft material of her pants leg, and he pulled back. That never should have come out of his mouth, but deep inside, he wanted to hear how she'd respond.

"Gabe, no. You're not weak." She reached for his hand as though she could somehow communicate better if she touched him. "I never should have said what I said."

He froze before he could pull away from her warm touch on his wrist.

Who was he kidding? She didn't even have to touch him. It had always been this way. When she was around, he forgot who he was. Even back in college, a glimpse of her walking into Bean and Gone or a text from her on his phone had put his heart in danger of a trip to the ER.

Funny how that was all coming back. It had only taken a few days for her to affect him. Their near-death experiences and near kisses hadn't helped to tamp down his emotions either. If anything, they'd intensified what he'd felt in the past.

They'd also made him reconsider the kind of man he wanted to be. He was no longer content to be the guy who shrank in the face of discomfort. He wanted to be the man who stood up for himself and for those he cared about, even if others didn't understand.

Might as well start now. He ran his right index finger along the edge of the swing. "Have you always been horrible at apologizing?"

"I'm sorry. What?"

When Hannah tilted her head to look at him, her red hair spilled over her shoulder, brushing her collarbone. Gabe reached over and pushed it back behind her ear, and his hand remained there. Her green eyes went wide. He hadn't meant to touch her. Yeah, it had crossed his mind that he'd like to, but he hadn't actually meant to *do* it.

"I…" He dropped his hand to the swing behind her shoulder. Maybe they could ignore it and resume their conversation.

What had they been talking about?

"I, um…" Hannah cleared her throat. "I apologized."

Gabe chuckled. She truly thought she had. "You can say the words *I'm sorry* in place of *excuse me* when you bump into someone, but you have a hard time saying *I'm sorry* by way of apology, don't you?"

She smiled as though she thought he was teasing

her, and maybe he was, but only a little. He did want to hear her say the words. To say them and to mean them.

"You sound like Zoe. She says I apologize with every word except *sorry*."

"Well, it's refreshing to hear you admit that."

Her smile faded. She turned toward him, bending one knee between them and planting one foot on the ground. Her shoulder brushed his hand, which still rested on the swing. When her green eyes met his, there was something different in them, something he'd caught a glimpse of at the gala but that had flared out so fast he'd thought he imagined it.

He wasn't imagining this.

Her shoulders rose as she inhaled. She never broke eye contact as she leaned closer. "I really am sorry." The words were barely a whisper, but it didn't seem as though it was from reluctance to say them.

It was almost as though something had taken her breath away.

Surely not him. Although his thumb brushing her shoulder and the narrow space between them was definitely making his own lungs work overtime.

When she didn't back away, he turned so that he faced her, mimicking her posture. If he was going to be a different man, one who took on new challenges, then he needed to start taking risks.

Risks like kissing Hannah Austin.

Slowly, giving her the chance to call a halt, Gabe slipped his hand to her shoulder and then to the back of her neck. When his fingers tangled in her hair, she leaned in, letting his gaze roam her face, her eyes, her lips…

He wasn't sure who closed the distance, but he felt the feather-soft brush of her lips against his…and then the heart-searing emotion of a years-long desire fulfilled as he finally kissed her the way he'd wanted to from the first time he'd seen her.

He'd known it would be like this. That she'd reach into his chest and own his heart. That he'd never want to breathe without her again. That she'd change his life in ways he couldn't put into words.

Ways he wasn't sure he'd ever recover from.

TWELVE

Hannah lost herself.

She forgot who she was. Forgot where she was. Forgot…everything. There was only Gabe and the novel feeling that she could stop controlling everything around her. She could simply exist right here, in this moment, with this man.

She was in her midtwenties again, crushing on Gabe in grad school, feeling as though—

With a gasp, she pulled away and scrambled back until she slammed into the arm of the swing and could go no farther.

She'd never been in grad school.

She'd been undercover then, and she was on the clock now. The truth about the past, about why she'd offered Gabe friendship so long ago, still hung between them. Although it had turned into more, at least for her, she'd used him to get to Trevor.

When he learned the truth…

Her hand went to her lips, still warm from his kiss. What had she done?

Gabe backed away as though she'd shoved him, his face immediately painted with regret. "Hannah, I'm sorry. I thought…"

"No." She reached for his hands and pulled them down to the swing between them. She shouldn't have kissed him…or let him kiss her. She wasn't really clear on how it had happened, but she couldn't let him think he'd violated her wishes. "You didn't do anything wrong. I…" Her eyes slipped shut. No way could she bear to look at him, not now. "I wanted you to."

His fingers tightened around hers. His exhale was loud enough to be heard over the wind that tousled the leaves on the trees.

She opened her eyes and stared at their laced fingers resting between them on the wooden slats of the swing. "We can't do this. It's too dangerous." She gently extracted her hand from his and stood.

It was *definitely* too dangerous. Because she didn't know how long they'd kissed, but for the entirety of that time, she'd been another person, someone she hadn't realized lived inside of her. Someone who let their guard down.

Gabe's attacker clearly knew where he lived. Anything could have happened while Hannah was preoccupied.

Anything.

She ran her tongue along the inside of her teeth, wanting to sit back down and kiss Gabe the way she'd always wanted to kiss him. To be held by him and to hold him in return. To be…safe.

When was the last time she'd felt safe? No matter how far back in her memory she went, there was no warm sense of security. From the time her mother had vanished when she was eleven, she'd been tasked with guarding her siblings while her father worked nights. Before that, her mother's volatile temper had kept everyone in the house on edge.

She'd joined the military to provide for her family. And when her father had died of a sudden heart attack shortly before the twins graduated from high school, she'd taken them in.

Safety wasn't a thing she'd ever thought could be hers, not until three minutes ago.

That was the problem. Safety was an illusion. It didn't exist in her world, especially not now. If she didn't do her job and uncover the truth of who was coming after Gabe, he may never know safety again.

As though he could read her thoughts, Gabe stood and backed a step away. "You're right. There's too much going on." That didn't sound like regret. It sounded like anger. He sniffed. "When it comes to me and you, there's always too much going on." Without looking back, he walked to the house, his posture straight and his head held high.

Hannah gripped the edge of the swing, pressing the weathered wood so hard that splinters dug into her palms.

Twice.

Twice her job had come between them. Twice her job had hurt him. Knowing he was wounded by the things she couldn't explain was almost more than she could take.

She turned her eyes to the sky. *Lord, I don't understand. Gabe doesn't deserve this. He deserves someone better than me. Help me to... I don't know. Help me to stop feeling things for him.*

That would make life so much easier. On every other mission and with every other man in her life, her heart had remained sealed. But with Gabe?

As safe as he was, he was also incredibly dangerous. Hannah leaned against the frame of the swing and glanced at her watch. She'd give Gabe ten minutes to get inside and get settled before she went in. She wasn't up to another encounter with him. It would either end in anger or another misguided kiss.

Neither was a good option.

She tipped her head and stared at stars so close she could count them through laced tree branches. On the side of the mountain, very little light pollution interfered with the view. As cliché as it was, she almost felt like she could reach up and take one out of the sky.

That was a fairytale thought, and fairytales didn't exist in the real world.

It was also the kind of thought that told her she'd been running too long without solid sleep or decent food. As much as she was certain she wouldn't rest, she needed to try. She'd spoken to Phillip earlier, and he'd likely be up all night sorting through the data from Skylark. He was more than capable of standing watch.

She started to move away from the swing, but motion near the corner of the house had her pressing her back against the heavy log support.

In the faint starlight, a shadow moved around the corner of the house from the garage. This was no stray cat or hungry bear waking up from a winter's slumber.

This was a man.

The figure was dressed in dark clothing, but it only served to make him stand out against the pale gray siding. From her spot in the shadows seventy-five feet from the house, Hannah watched silently, calculating her next move. There was no good way to sneak up on the figure. She'd have to cross open lawn to get there quickly. Keeping to the fringes around the edges of the yard pretty much guaranteed she'd rustle dry leaves and twigs.

She slipped her hand to the thigh pocket of her leggings, going for her phone to alert Phillip and Thalia.

Empty.

Had she really left her phone in the house? With her pistol secured in a lockbox inside, she was unarmed and on her own.

The figure paused by the back door and seemed to be listening. Keeping close to the wall, he crouched to stay below the kitchen window and the hall bathroom window.

He was heading for Gabe's room.

The only thing she had going for her was that Phillip and Gabe were both awake. Shouting would alert everyone inside and bring them running. It would also scare the trespasser.

But with the element of surprise, she might be able to catch him before he got too far away. She could end this tonight. Restore Gabe's life. Maybe even let them—

No. She couldn't think beyond setting Gabe's life back in order. As long as she had to keep her past reasons for getting to know him a secret, they could never be more than friends.

They shouldn't even be that.

Hannah balled her fists, easing away from the swing to make her way slowly toward the house.

Rolling her feet from heel to toe as she walked, Hannah took the long route along the edge of the yard, trying to avoid leaves and twigs that would alert the prowler to her presence. The gap narrowed. Fifty feet. Forty-five. Forty.

At Gabe's window, the shadow rose and pressed something to the glass.

Her eyebrow arched. This was a new level of sophistication if the guy was using a glass cutter.

She stepped again.

A twig snapped.

The figure froze and spun in her direction. His hair was covered by the hood of a sweatshirt, and his face was hidden behind a ski mask. With a muffled curse, he turned and bolted for the street.

Hannah ran after him. "Gabe! Phillip!" She called their names as she raced across the yard, shouting until her voice was hoarse. The effort cost her air and speed, but she kept running.

Gabe's bedroom light came on as she reached the house. The suspect was in her sights until he rounded the corner.

She nearly bolted into the front yard without pausing but stopped just before she exposed her position. Pressing against the siding, she crouched and eased forward to peer into the front yard.

A bullet cracked into the siding as the sound of a gunshot broke the stillness of the night.

She jerked back into hiding.

A dog started barking somewhere down the mountain road. Shouts came from inside the house. Light poured from windows.

She peeked again, but the shadow was gone. The sound of an engine and spinning tires on gravel spit the news of the man's getaway into the dark night.

Hannah had failed.

Gabe balled his fists at his sides and resisted the urge to put one of them through the siding where a small hole revealed a bullet's entry.

A bullet that had been fired at Hannah.

He dragged his hand through his hair and stepped away from Phillip, who was shining a flashlight into the jagged hole. He wore latex gloves he'd pulled from a kit in his backpack.

Every outside floodlight was on as well as all of the inside lights, turning his normally dark property into the mountain equivalent of an airport runway.

Great. His house was a crime scene. Again. He puffed air out and balled his fists even tighter. At some point, this had to stop. He just wasn't sure what *the end* would look like.

Phillip glanced at him and seemed to weigh his thoughts. Finally, he turned back to his work. "I think I can get to the bullet without doing more damage to your siding. I may have to trim a bit though. You have tools in the garage?"

"Yeah. Whatever you need."

From the backyard, the rise and fall of Thalia and Hannah's conversation drifted to him. They were combing the area with flashlights, searching for things he didn't even want to imagine.

Phillip straightened and faced him. "You okay, man?"

"I'm angry." The words surprised him. He'd planned to say "fine" or "all good," but the truth he hadn't even realized found its way out. When it did, the emotion raged behind it. "Furious."

"Yeah, the clenched fists sort of gave you away."

Gabe flexed his fingers, shocked by how stiff they felt. He must have had them balled up tighter than he'd thought. His shoulders and neck were in knots as well.

He'd have to live with it. The stress wasn't going away anytime soon. "This is why you all do what you do, isn't it?"

"Anger? No. That will just get you into trouble."

"Not anger." That wasn't what he'd meant. In his

spun-up state, he couldn't even seem to get words out properly. "Someone has torn down my life from the outside, and now they want to come in and rip it apart from the inside. That hit-and-run deal on post? That was a warning shot. Something to let me know I was seen, wasn't it?"

Phillip merely watched, his lips a tight line.

Gabe paced away a few feet, eyeing the side of the house. The outdoor house lights created fleeting shadows as Thalia and Hannah searched the backyard. "Then they wrecked my identity. That was just to be mean. Now they want me dead. They want me to know I have no control. Am I right?" He turned toward Phillip, digging his fists into his hips. He'd never profiled an unknown person before, but the pieces all fit.

"What else are you thinking?"

"That they want to be seen, or at least they did at first. The truck, the identity hack… Those were things to get noticed. The carbon monoxide, the sniper, this?" He shook his head. "Also, they aren't after Hannah. She's just the one who keeps…" The fire turned to ash in his veins, leaving him cold. "She's the one who keeps getting between them and me." Hannah kept stepping into danger for him, literally standing between him and a bullet more than once. "It's personal when it comes to me. It's removing an obstacle when it comes to her."

"Collateral damage." Phillip's voice was low. He shut off his flashlight and shoved it into his pocket, deepening the shadows around them. "Gabe, I can't speak for Thalia or Hannah, but I do this because of what you're feeling right now. Justice. Protection. The sense that I have to do something because I can't simply stand by with my hands in my pockets and watch."

"I can't either. Not anymore." He'd seen the ugly in

the world in ways he'd never imagined. Before, he'd been taunted. Now he was being hunted. Innocent people could get in the way of something meant to harm him. He couldn't let that stand.

Hannah was right. His skills could be put to better use bringing down lowlifes like whoever was doing this to him.

To Hannah.

"I see the wheels turning in your head. You're a good profiler. You'd be an asset to any team." Phillip offered a brief smile before he tugged his gloves tighter onto his fingers. "You already think like an investigator. But, Gabe?"

"What?"

Switching on his flashlight, Phillip crouched to study the bullet hole again. "Be careful. What you're feeling now is personal. It's emotional. It may not be a calling. But if it is? Working with someone you have feelings for can be very…problematic." The words sounded heavy, like more than a warning.

The back of Gabe's neck heated. "I don't—"

"Guys?" Hannah's voice from the backyard cut off what would likely be him protesting too much. Phillip was smart. He knew there were emotions simmering between Gabe and Hannah.

As Gabe turned toward her voice, Hannah appeared at the corner of the house. "We found something."

Slinging his backpack over his shoulder, Phillip scooted past Gabe and headed for the women, who stood together in the backyard.

Gabe followed, keeping his gaze away from Hannah. The floodlights that hung from his eaves cast harsh light onto the scene, and he couldn't bear to look her in the face, not after what had happened between them on that swing.

Not after what Phillip had indicated he suspected.

Thalia walked to the space beneath Gabe's window, where footprints had broken taller grass that would soon need to be mowed. She turned her flashlight to the base of a box hedge.

Something glinted in the beam.

Phillip crouched, opened his backpack and produced a plastic evidence bag. "You took a photo already?"

"Yes." Hannah's voice came from over Gabe's shoulder. "You can bag it. I'm guessing our guy dropped it when he figured out I was headed for him."

When he rose, Phillip held out his gloved hand. A small glass bottle with a red-and-white label rested in his palm. *Xylazine*.

Thalia muttered words Gabe probably shouldn't try to interpret.

Hannah huffed behind him. "Now we know."

"Know what?" Gabe turned to her as Phillip stowed the evidence in the bag. "What's xylazine?" He asked the question, but his queasy stomach said he didn't want to know the answer.

"Horse tranquilizer." Hannah met his gaze without flinching, her expression impassive. It was pretty clear she'd stepped back from any emotional involvement and was in investigative mode. "Not hard to purchase online. Easier to obtain than fentanyl. Takes more to cause…" She hesitated and glanced at Thalia with a rare flash of uncertainty.

Thalia took over. "It's lethal in high doses, but it's also a beast at lower doses. Unlike fentanyl, it doesn't respond to emergency treatment with naloxone, which we all carry. It really doesn't respond well to anything."

Her explanation probably should have terrified him, but Gabe simply felt numb. He'd been through so many near misses that this one rolled off his back in a way that scared him. It scared him because it *didn't* upset him. Later, when he turned out the lights, he'd probably feel differently, but for now, he was simply in his head, with his emotions disengaged. "It's definitely personal."

Hannah stepped away, staring at the swing that stood at the edge of the floodlights. What was she thinking?

"This is different than shooting at you." Thalia was still taking lead. "This is an in-your-face kind of thing. They'd have to get close. Actually touch you."

"Actually look me in the face. I was right." He turned to Phillip. "It's personal."

Phillip didn't look up from where he was writing on the bag, but he gave a curt nod.

"I wonder though…" Hannah's voice broke the silence that hung among them. She turned toward their small circle. "How dead do they want him?"

Thalia's head jerked back. "There's only one kind of dead."

"Yeah, but if they wanted him *dead* dead, he'd already be that way."

Gabe's stomach clinched. It was bizarre being talked about as though he wasn't standing right there. It was even more bizarre hearing talk about his own death.

Hannah stepped closer. "I think this is about your software. That's come up more than once. You say only you know about it, yet it's in a lot of people's mouths."

That was true.

Shoving the evidence into his backpack, Phillip joined the conversation. "The hit-and-run could have been a warning shot. They'd have struck him if they really wanted to."

Hannah nodded slowly. "The shootings on the road and at Skylark could have been panicked, last-ditch attempts to keep us from uncovering something by talking to Trevor or by logging into Skylark's system."

"What about the carbon monoxide?" When the last word cracked slightly, Gabe cleared his throat. "That says *dead* to me."

"Or incapacitated." Hannah tipped her head toward Phillip's backpack. "True, in large doses, xylazine is lethal. But in smaller doses, it causes disorientation, dizziness, or nervous system depression."

"So if this is tied to the software…" Phillip sucked air through his teeth, his expression shifting to one of understanding, as though he'd picked up on Hannah's train of thought. "It could be that they don't want him dead, but they want him to talk, to tell where he's hidden the software."

Hannah pointed at him. "Exactly. Gabe's worth more to them alive, at least for the moment. If they kill him outright, they can't get the location of the software from him. Once they get that, they'll probably—"

"I'm standing right here." Gabe held up his hands. While he might be numb, he wasn't immune to panic at the clinical discussion of his own murder.

"Sorry." Hannah winced and shot him a silent apology. "I forget you're not an agent used to brainstorming on the fly."

"He was doing a pretty good job earlier." At a slight buzzing sound, Phillip reached into his pocket, excused himself and stepped away from the group to answer the phone.

Thalia followed.

Hannah's eyebrow arched, but she didn't pursue Phillip's comment. Instead, she watched the pair standing several feet away, sharing the phone.

Hmm. That thing Phillip had said about being involved with colleagues might be—

"Gabe? What's Phillip talking about?" Hannah swung her gaze to him.

"Later." He wasn't ready to discuss what was stirring in him. He wanted to sleep on it. Pray about it. To heed Phillip's warning and get out of this constant adrenaline rush before he committed to major life changes.

Assuming he'd have a life to change when this was over.

"Fair enough." In the light, Hannah looked tired. The shadows under her eyes were deep. When was the last time she'd slept? "But we need to talk about—"

"Guys?" Phillip cut in, jogging back with Thalia on his heels. He somehow managed to look both grim and excited. "That was Dana. She's found something, and I think it might help us finally put an end to this."

THIRTEEN

Hannah had never known a more tense two hours than the drive from Asheville to the far side of Gatlinburg, Tennessee. They'd rolled out at dawn, so while the day was still young, she was already exhausted.

Their winding course had her gripping the steering wheel and watching the rearview mirror, chased by memories of their last run through the mountains and the gunshots that had nearly killed them. She could usually endure a trauma like that and move forward, compartmentalizing it in the darkest parts of her mind. Thanks to being raised without a mother figure in her life, she'd often been accused of reacting and thinking more like a man than a woman. Then again, Thalia was the same way, so maybe it was training.

She gripped the steering wheel tighter. Stress and lack of sleep had her mind all over the place. Rolling her shoulders, she tried to relax, taking note of Thalia and Phillip as they came around a curve behind them.

No way was she going it alone this time.

Gabe had been silent for most of the drive, sitting stiffly in the seat as though he was also having trouble relaxing. Was it because they'd kissed? Or because the fact that he was a target had finally sunk in? Either way, she couldn't endure the silence any longer.

"What's got you so quiet?"

For the first time since he'd snapped his seat belt into place, he looked at her.

She turned her attention back to the road. Looking him in the eye made her want to search for that same expression he'd worn last night right before he'd—

Hannah cleared her throat. *Focus*.

Gabe shifted, drumming his fingers on his knees. "I want to work for you."

That was the last thing she'd expected. She whipped her head toward him before she remembered she was driving. "You want to what?"

"If the offer's still good, I want to take you and your shadow organization up on it." His voice was firm, resolute.

If it was anyone else, she'd write this off as a knee-jerk reaction to the happenings of the past few days. But this was Gabe Buchanan. He thought things through. Lined possibilities into neat rows. Plotted and planned.

Still, he wasn't immune to reacting like anyone else would.

And she was no longer certain that having him on her team was right. The danger he'd faced on a daily basis since she'd walked back into his life was making her increasingly uncomfortable. It was stealing her sleep on a mission that would be stressful even if she wasn't constantly waking up from dreams about a future with Gabe.

"We can talk about that later." She offered him a nod as she lifted her foot from the accelerator and hit the turn signal to make a right onto a side road. "There are a lot of hoops to jump through. This is a highly sensitive position. It will require security clearance and that can take a while to complete. The training is—"

"Are you trying to talk me out of it?" His voice was a toxic blend of confusion and anger. "You were the one who—"

"It's not that. It's just that we're almost there." She pointed at the GPS. "Like I said, we'll discuss it later. Right now, we have bigger things to worry about."

"Sure." Gabe leaned forward and eyed the narrow road that wound up the mountain. "This doesn't look like we're headed for a software development firm. More like a backwoods date with the business end of somebody's shotgun."

"I'm thinking the same thing." Dana's deep-records dive had uncovered a grant request made to the Science and Technology Directorate of the Department of Homeland Security. A company called HuntLab, LLC had applied for a grant to develop software that sounded stunningly similar to Gabe's profiling program.

Too similar.

The grant application was in process, and the address pointed to this site outside Gatlinburg. They'd done satellite recon, but the thick trees made it difficult to discern more than a single structure on the property at the address.

Hannah had been prepared to search the backwoods of Tennessee, but seeing the route play out in real time made the hair on her arms stand up. This didn't look right. They could be driving into a trap.

She shouldn't have brought Gabe, but she needed him to ask the deeper questions and to verify if the program in question was actually his or if there was a genuine researcher out there who'd simply had a similar idea.

"You still don't know who could have told anyone

else about your software?" That was what kept nagging her. If Dr. Donovan Mathison was truly Gabe's only confidant and the man had told no one, this secret should have died with him. "Are you sure Dr. Mathison was trustworthy? He wouldn't sell the intel to someone else?"

"No. I mean, yes, he was trustworthy. We came to the conclusion together that it was an ethical issue and it needed to be shelved. He never had a copy. He helped me work out some knots, but he never had enough of the work to duplicate it. We never spoke of it outside of his office, because I knew from the start it would demand some level of secrecy. Unless his office was bugged?" He glanced at her with an arched eyebrow.

Anything was possible, though her understanding of Dr. Mathison's work suggested it would never have commanded scrutiny from outside parties. "Was he into anything under the radar? Something he couldn't talk about?"

Gabe pinched his lips together and shook his head. "He was constantly inventing things, and he put a lot of money into prototypes and patents, but none of it was software. He was a car guy and was all about engines and drive trains."

Money could have motivated him to sell, but nothing in Mathison's profiles indicated he and his wife were in dire straits. She'd have Dana check again.

"We could talk to his widow one more time. It may be time to tell her everything. It might spark a memory that could help us." She eased off the gas and cruised slowly past the head of a driveway that wound back to a cabin barely visible through the trees. The cabin and drive appeared to be tidy and cared for, but they were small and nestled in a thickly wooded area that afforded few ways to pull surveillance.

Her car chirped as Phillip called, and she answered with the Bluetooth. "Let me guess... Since I don't see you behind me, I'm assuming you've pulled off the road, and you and Thalia are headed down to surveil the cabin? You'll take up a position at the rear in case we get a runner?"

"Spot-on. Just didn't want you to shoot us when you catch us creeping through the woods. Give us two minutes to get into place."

"Got it." She killed the call and drove past the cabin, searching for a spot wide enough to do a three-point turn so they could circle back.

"Do you guys always read each other's thoughts that way?" Gabe was studying the trees out the passenger window as though the question wasn't important.

She had a feeling it was though. "The three of us have worked together before. When you've done this long enough, you learn people's habits and their skill sets, and you start to guess what they're going to do." She found a short drive and turned into it, then backed out onto the road. "It's the nature of the beast that is this job."

He cut her a look, but before he could speak, the phone rang again.

Saved by the literal bell. Hannah punched the button. "You set?"

"Yes. Appears to be a small one-bedroom place. One person visible inside, and we have eyes on him. White male. Looks to be about thirty. Brown hair. Blue Henley. Jeans. One vehicle outside around the back. Late 2010s Chevy SUV. Red. Thalia's covering it."

"We're on, then. Switching to comms. Let me know

if he makes a sudden move." Hannah pulled slowly into the driveway, grateful her SUV looked more like a mom-mobile than a made-for-TV, tinted-window government monster. Fitting her earpiece in place, she hesitated before passing the case to Gabe. "Wear this and wait in the car. If anything goes south, get out of here."

"No. I want to hear this guy out. If I—"

Surely he wasn't arguing with her now. "My job is first and foremost to protect you. Finding out who's doing this to you is secondary. If you're out there with me, I can't do job one."

"And if you're out there, you can't protect me in here."

She flinched. Her failures glared at her every time she looked in the mirror or closed her eyes. He didn't have to poke that wound. The op was out of control. She already knew—

The door to the cabin opened, and the man that Phillip had described stepped out and studied their SUV.

Gabe leaned forward, staring out the window. "Hannah? We might have a problem."

"What's the problem?" Hannah reached over and laid her hand against Gabe's chest, shoving him away from the windshield.

How would that help?

He bristled. All she'd done was shove him aside like he was a wimp who couldn't take care of himself. She threw all sorts of knots into his self-esteem.

The more she did it, the more he wanted to prove he was the opposite of who she thought he was. But that wasn't important right now, because he was staring at a ghost.

Almost.

Hunter Mathison was a carbon copy of his late father, although his face carried fewer laugh lines. It was clear that a life path littered with drugs and alcohol had taken a toll. Still, there was no denying who he was.

"What's the problem?" Phillip's voice in Gabe's earpiece echoed Hannah's question and slapped Gabe back into the moment. If he didn't answer, someone might go in with guns raised.

"I only met him once, but I'm pretty sure that's the Mathisons' estranged son."

Hannah opened the car door. "Stay here."

She approached Hunter slowly as he walked down the steps into the yard.

Gabe studied him. Hunter appeared to be relaxed, not stressed or on guard. In the woods to the left, Phillip was watching. They were as safe as they could be. Gabe was going in, despite Hannah's wishes. He had questions. Easing out of the truck, he watched Hannah before he approached.

She reached into her inside jacket pocket and removed the wallet that held her credentials. "Are you Hunter Mathison?"

For the first time, Hunter looked wary. "Who's asking?"

Hannah flashed her badge. "Chief Warrant Officer Hannah Austin, US Army special investigations."

"What's the Army want with me? I haven't done anything wrong." The sideways skitter of his gaze said differently.

Gabe recognized that expression. While the bulk of his experience was reading online data, he'd learned to profile physical behavior as well. This man was scared…and guilty of something.

For the first time, Hunter noticed Gabe. He froze. It seemed as if time stopped.

Then he bolted…straight toward Phillip, who stepped out of the tree line with his gun pointed at the ground.

That was enough to bring Hunter to a skidding halt, nearly crashing face-first into the leaves scattered along the ground. He righted himself and held his hands up, though no one had commanded him to.

He whirled toward Hannah and Gabe, his stare fixed on Gabe. "What do you want?" His voice was frantic. "I don't have the journals. I can't stop what…what Trevor started."

"What Trevor started?" Hannah pocketed her ID as she walked to Hunter. She said something to him that Gabe couldn't hear and then stood aside as Phillip patted him down. When she was satisfied he wasn't a danger, she shot a fiery look at Gabe.

Fine. His presence had escalated the situation, but he had a right to hear what Hunter had to say.

"Talk to me about Trevor Haskell." Hannah slipped her hands into her pockets as though this was a casual conversation between friends, likely trying to lure Hunter into a false sense of ease.

He glanced at Gabe, whose presence seemed to make him skittish. "You're Gabe Buchanan, right?"

Hannah stepped between them. "You address me, not him. I asked you a question you have yet to answer. Are you Hunter Mathison?"

Hunter dragged his gaze back to Hannah. "Yes. Is he Buchanan?"

"Why?"

"Because he's here to kill me." Hunter's gaze flicked to Gabe again.

That was definitely fear. Gabe knew what it felt like

to fear someone who could harm you. Making someone else feel that sting didn't sit well with him. He eased to the right so he could be seen. "Why would I want to kill you?"

"Because I told Haskell about your program and how you were the one who told the feds about him."

What? Gabe held up both hands as though he was surrendering. That information knocked him a step backward. "You were out of the picture by the time I started working with your dad. What makes you say that?"

Hannah stepped to the side, keeping a careful eye on Hunter but letting Gabe take the wheel. Hunter seemed to be more inclined to talk openly to Gabe than he'd been to talk to her, so she was probably letting this proceed naturally instead of butting in.

She was still going to have some choice words for him later, no doubt.

"I was a second stringer on the basketball team in high school when Trevor was a starter. I knew him a little after he moved back for grad school. He was at a few parties, always had the money to liven things up with the good stuff."

Gabe fought not to react. *The good stuff?* He'd known Trevor drank, but this sounded like more than that, especially given that Hunter Mathison had a known drug problem. "Define *good stuff.*"

For moment, Hunter stared at Hannah, seeming to consider something before he cursed, his lips twisted in disgust. "Know what? Trevor ratted me out to you guys, so I might as well…" He threw up his hands. "We partied with what college kids could afford, you know? But Trevor? He'd bring the high-dollar stuff. Cocaine. High-grade marijuana. Oxy, even after the price shot up.

Trevor elevated a party because he always had money nobody else had."

The money Trevor had pocketed from extorting a senator had obviously bought him popularity.

His earpiece crackled with Thalia's voice. She was still out of sight, Hannah's ace in the hole if things went sideways. "Ask him if Trevor was using. The more he spills, the more likely we can keep Trevor in jail even if he beats the extortion."

Gabe's stomach shriveled. Here he was again, in the position to keep his former best friend behind bars. Although, if Hunter was telling the truth, Trevor had lied to him.

He relayed the question, the words bile in his mouth.

"Nah. He was the big-time athlete. Wouldn't risk it. That's why he was a starter and I wasn't." Hunter seemed to shrug off the effects addiction had wreaked on his life.

"Tell me why you think I'd want to kill you." Gabe was tired of talking about Trevor's past. He wanted today's truth, which Trevor had failed to tell them. "What does Trevor know?"

"Is this off-the-record?" Hunter looked at Hannah. "Because I kind of like living like a free man here and not next door to Trevor in prison."

"I'll tell you what." Hannah widened her stance and planted her hands on her hips, shifting from friendly conversationalist to authoritative cop mode. "You answer our questions, and I won't go to the judge for a warrant to search your place."

Hunter blanched.

Thalia snickered in his ear. "You know you have no probable cause, right?"

Hannah didn't flinch. She knew that, but Hunter

didn't. "What do you say, Mathison? A few answers, and we walk away without taking a walk through your house."

Hunter looked as though he could kick himself for ever walking out the front door. His shoulders sagged. "Fine. But nothing I say came from me. Trevor's not a killer, but I'm not so sure about anyone else who's involved."

Shoving his hands into his pockets, Gabe tried to hold his temper. Hunter Mathison was nothing like his father, who'd been kind and selfless almost to a fault. Junior here was as selfish as he could be and was a twisting nightmare in conversation.

Gabe tipped his head to look over the cabin, watching the wind ruffle the leaves of the trees that sheltered the place. "Clearly, this isn't the high-tech industry hub the government thinks it is." As soon as he said the words, he dropped his chin, looking to Hannah. Speaking was probably the last thing he should have done.

She said nothing.

Hunter smirked. "I saw a way to make a few bucks, no harm done."

"Let's talk about that grant. You came up with the software idea?" Hannah was wresting control back from Gabe.

Something that might be pain skittered across Hunter's face, as though Hannah's question had snagged an exposed nerve. "A few months ago, I needed some cash, so I went back to the house while I knew my mother would be at work."

Gabe balled his fists in his pockets. Hunter had stolen from his mother? In the wake of his father's death?

"I found Dad's journals. He brain-dumped everything in those books. He'd write down stuff he was thinking about or working on or was, you know, praying about or whatever." Hunter shrugged, though it wasn't as nonchalant as he likely wanted it to look. "I grabbed a couple of them, thinking there might be something useful in there, something I could use to take a page out of Trevor's playbook, ya know?"

"You were looking for blackmail material? You thought you might get lucky and find some secrets your dad knew about others?" Hannah had the look that said she was putting pieces together. "You found something different instead." She glanced over her shoulder at Gabe. "Did you know about these journals?"

Gabe shook his head. *No.* But if Dr. Mathison had written about his work, that would explain so much.

"Whatever," Hunter spat the word, eyeing Gabe with open contempt. "He replaced me with you. Wrote about how you were the son he wished I'd turned out to be."

Gabe clamped down on his tongue. Hunter had chosen drugs over his family. He'd vanished when they tried to put him in rehab, long before Gabe ever came on the scene.

It almost looked as though Hunter was going to spit at Gabe's feet. "That's why I had no problem doing what I did."

"And what did you do?" Hannah's voice was almost soothing, like she sympathized with his actions.

Gabe strained inside his skin, wishing she'd force Hunter to just get to the point.

"He went on and on about some software Gabe had developed. How it was ahead of its time, and what a genius the wonder boy was. So I thought, hey, the government is always giving out grants to people to develop stuff. Figured I'd pitch them Gabe's idea, tell them I was working on it, rake in the money, then tell them it didn't pan out."

Hannah nodded. "What's Trevor's role?"

"Dad wrote how he was praying for Gabe with everything that had happened with Trevor. It didn't take much to figure out that Gabe was behind the anonymous tip that busted him. I made a phone call and let Trevor know what I'd found, asked if he wanted to buy the journals. He said no, but he thanked me for the information. Said he could use it. Not long after that, somebody offered me big bucks for those journals. I figured, why not? What good were they to me at that point if Trevor didn't want to pay for them?"

"Who offered the money?"

Hunter shrugged. "I don't know. We did the whole spy-show thing. I got the money out of a trash can on a hiking trail not far from here. Left the journals behind. That was about six weeks ago. End of story."

As the wind in the trees picked up, Gabe looked over at Phillip, who was watching him with a mixture of curiosity and pity, probably picking up on his restlessness.

Trevor had lied to his face in that prison interview room.

And that meant his former best friend might be the man who was trying to kill him.

FOURTEEN

Gabe sat on the weight bench and stared at the white cinder-block wall in his basement. He'd intended to work out his frustration on the treadmill since Hannah had banned him from running the roads without an armed escort, but once he'd hit the bottom of the stairs, his energy had evaporated.

Truthfully, he was hiding from Hannah, who was upstairs going over Hunter's statement with Thalia and Phillip.

She was angry Gabe had interfered. So angry that he'd opted to ride back with Phillip. He didn't want to hear what she had to say. He was tired of being bossed around and questioned and viewed as weak.

So weak that she'd basically rescinded her job offer.

He'd been sitting for ten minutes, counting the blocks in the wall. He felt caged. Every move was watched. Worse, it felt as though he was being spied on by someone he couldn't even see. Although they'd made it safely to Gatlinburg and back, the trip had been an exercise in fear and dread.

He kept waiting for the sucker punch, just like he had in middle school. Back then, he couldn't eat or sleep. He'd fallen into pits so low he'd never talked to anyone about them except the counselor his parents had finally forced him to see. He'd felt helpless and useless, weak and targeted.

Kind of like now.

Lifting his chin toward the paneled ceiling, he closed his eyes. *Come on, God. I'm a grown man. I shouldn't feel like a twelve-year-old who just got his backpack dropped into the toilet. Again. People respect me now.*

Or did they?

Coworkers might. Clients might.

Hannah didn't.

She'd talked so smoothly right before she kissed him, but that had been short-lived.

He stood and walked to the counter in the corner where a mini fridge held water and protein shakes. He grabbed a bottle of water and stared at his work phone where it lay on the counter, powered off. He'd dropped it there before they left for Gatlinburg. Hannah thought it was a bad idea to carry it when they were away from the house. Too easy to track.

But he was home now, where his would-be killer clearly felt safe to visit, and this might be his ticket to regaining some control. To feel like he was helping someone instead of being a helpless mess.

He owed it to Jeanette Mathison to tell her they'd found her prodigal son, that he seemed well, although Gabe had no doubt he was still using.

It might tear open wounds in a woman who hadn't seen her son since his brief appearance at her husband's funeral, but it felt irresponsible to say nothing.

Powering up the phone, Gabe scrolled through his contacts and pressed the screen, feeling like a guilty teenager who'd been grounded and was sneaking a call.

Jeanette answered on the first ring. "Gabe. I'm so

glad to hear from you." Her voice held relief that caught him in the chest. He hadn't considered she'd be worried after their initial conversation and their short conversation the day before. "I've tried to call your phone all day, but it goes straight to voice mail."

"That's a story I'll have to tell another time." He didn't feel like rehashing the past few days, not even with the woman who was like his second mother. All he wanted was to pass along his news and help Mrs. Mathison deal with the fallout.

It was better to just say it than to draw it out. "I saw Hunter today." He winced and waited.

The line was silent, and then she sighed. "I assume he's still near Gatlinburg?"

"You know?" The last time she'd spoken of Hunter, several months earlier, she'd been clueless to his whereabouts.

"Yes. I choose to keep my distance for fear he'll take off for someplace I can't find him." Her voice was matter-of-fact, as though she'd long ago worked through the negative emotions about her son. "Several months ago, Hunter came into the house when I wasn't home. He took some of his father's journals. I assume he was searching for passwords or account information. He also took some jewelry he probably thought I wouldn't miss. He didn't know I had installed security cameras after his father died."

Should he tell her what Hunter had done with those journals? He chewed on the words and then swallowed them. The investigation was ongoing. There was also no reason to pile on to her pain. "I'm sorry."

"It's been a lot of years, and I hold out hope that…" The pause stretched, as though she was trying to gather her thoughts. "I hired a private investigator after the break-in. I wanted to know he was safe. The PI keeps me apprised of his whereabouts. At least I know where he is. I also know that addiction still has him in a python's grip, but until he's ready to admit there's a problem, there's nothing I can do. I want to put him in rehab again, one that has a stellar success rate, but... Well... These things often take more than we have to offer." Her voice was steely.

What would it be like to have a child whose addiction led him to turn his back on the parents who loved him? Who stole and lied and hid? "I'm sorry." *Again.* What else could he say?

"Anyway... How did you see him? He's not in town, is he?"

This was where it got tricky. Much of what was happening was likely secret due to the investigation, and he certainly couldn't share that Hunter was involved in what was happening to him. "I can't say, but he was sober."

"That's good." She sounded relieved, as though his news had released some tension. "He's not a bad person. He just needs help."

Maybe he wasn't, but stealing from his parents, lying to the government and searching for ways to extort money were all tough to excuse, even if Hunter was in the throes of an addiction he couldn't defeat.

"Well." Mrs. Mathison's voice snapped across the line with a zing that said she was purposely changing the subject. "When do I get to see you? You usually show up for dinner at least once a month. You're overdue."

Gabe smiled. "As soon as this storm in my life blows over, I'll drop by. In fact—"

"I'm concerned about this 'storm' you're in. It sounds

dangerous. I still have space here if you need a safe place to hide."

It was tempting. "I'm fine and in good hands. If I—"

Footsteps on the stairs stopped him. They were quick and sounded like running shoes.

Most likely Hannah. Thalia was a fan of boots, he'd noticed, probably because they made her feel taller and therefore more powerful.

Sometimes, he couldn't turn the profiling off.

Sure enough, Hannah appeared at the foot of the stairs, her frown deepening when she saw his phone.

"Gabe?" Mrs. Mathison sounded concerned.

"I'm sorry." Would he ever stop saying that? "I have to go. I have a meeting." They said their goodbyes, and he disconnected the call, powering down the device to avoid looking Hannah in the eye.

"Was that Jeanette Mathison?" An eerie calm layered over her anger. It was a tone he was growing to dislike.

"It was." Gabe shoved the phone into the pocket of his running shorts as he stood to face her. She might have the authority in the investigation, but he had the height advantage. That fact was petty and meant nothing, but it kept him from feeling completely powerless.

Hannah pinned him with a hard gaze, one that he couldn't look away from. "You told her about Hunter? You never should have done that. This is an active investigation and you could—"

Enough. "Would you stop, please?" His words weren't loud, but the force behind them bounced off the wall in a way that made Hannah snap her mouth shut. "I'm not seven years old. I'm also not stupid. I may not be as well-trained as you are, but I'm an adult. I said nothing that would compromise your investigation. In fact, she already knew where Hunter was."

"Did you tell her—"

"I merely told her that her son was alive, and that he was safe, at least for now. I wasn't going to keep that from her." He stepped closer, the burn in his chest making it hard to breathe.

But it wasn't anger. It was disappointment. The sting of once again seeing how she felt about him. "You think I'm weak. Possibly even stupid. You denied it outside last night, but you do. You think I can't hack this. That's why you're backing down about letting me on your team. I'm not good enough for you. "Not personally and not professionally either. I wasn't good enough for you in grad school, and I'm not now."

"Gabe." Her expression melted, and she stepped closer. "That's not—"

"Don't." He couldn't listen to her say things that ran contrary to her actions. Not anymore.

Without getting within arm's reach, he stepped around her and walked up the stairs. He wasn't sure where he was going, but he was certain it was far away from Hannah Austin.

Hannah jumped when the door at the top of the stairs slammed.

Let him go. It's better this way. Better if they didn't continue this dance around each other. Better if Gabe didn't work for Overwatch. Better if she wrapped up this investigation and walked away. She'd lived her life without him for years, and she'd return to her life without him once this was over.

Except she'd thought about him nearly every day since Trevor had been taken into custody and she'd walked away. She'd kept tabs on how he was doing.

That was why his was the first name to pop into her head when she needed a profiler and tech consultant.

But it would never work. Their history was too complicated. Their personalities and life experiences were too different. While he'd been bullied, he'd grown up with a loving family around him.

Her upbringing had included an abusive-and-then-absent mother and a father who depended on her to care for her siblings. She'd always been the adult. The responsible one. The one who stood between danger and the prey it sought.

It seemed Gabe was intent on running around her protection.

So were Eli and Zoe.

She settled on the weight bench that Gabe had vacated and pulled her phone from her pocket. She hadn't talked to Zoe since that little blowout they'd had, and she had no way to reach Eli since he was locked down in the Q Course.

She'd never gone this long without reaching out to her siblings, and she had no idea what to say to a sister who'd made a move Hannah viewed as foolish.

God, help me speak with love. Hannah punched the numbers on the screen and waited for the call to connect. They needed to talk this out.

It was four rings before Zoe answered. "If you're calling to yell, I'm not interested."

The words cut Hannah through the heart. If there was a wedge between them, she'd driven it there with her reaction to Zoe's news. "I'm sorry. I didn't handle that phone call well the other night." She could say that there was a lot going on or that she was stressed, but Zoe didn't need excuses.

She needed her sister to listen.

"I'm going to need you to repeat that," Zoe said. "I'd like to record it, because you so rarely apologize."

Hannah bit her tongue. She'd said she was sorry. She didn't need to be reamed about it.

"Okay, that was too far, I get it. But it was surprising." Zoe didn't sound apologetic. She did sound subdued though. "Are you getting soft in your old age?"

"I'm not old." Although after the past few days, she sure felt like it. "Although I guess I *am* a few years ahead of you, young lady. I wish you would have talked to me before you decided to get married." It was such a leap to make without consulting with her big sister. "That's a huge life decision. Bigger than you—"

"And there it is." Zoe sighed.

"There's what?" Standing, Hannah paced to the kitchenette and stole a water from Gabe's fridge. She couldn't sit still. There was too much happening. The attacks on Gabe. Her sister's marriage. Eli's insistence on running into the world's most dangerous job.

She couldn't protect any of them.

"*There's what?* How about there's you thinking you have the lock on wisdom because you're older. Treating me like I'm a child."

"You are a—" *Child.* Had she really almost said that to her twenty-year-old sister?

Everything Gabe had said to her on the drive to the prison rushed back.

This time, it sank in. The realization of her arrogance and control issues weakened her knees. She dropped to the weight bench, speechless.

"You finally heard yourself, didn't you?" Zoe asked. She'd always been intuitive. "Sis, you signed up for the Army at eighteen so you could provide for us. You were working undercover when you weren't much older than me. It's time you realized I'm not a child. Neither is Eli."

Hannah sank against the slanted back of the weight bench. Now that she'd *heard herself*, she could also hear dozens of other things she'd said throughout the years. "It's hard, Zo." An ache lodged deep in her throat. For her whole life, Zoe and Eli had been her responsibility. Now they were taking the reins of their own lives as adults.

Where did that leave her?

"I know." Zoe's voice was thick with the tears that Hannah herself refused to shed. "You had to take on so much when we were too small to do it ourselves. You've always been the responsible one. But you and Dad did your jobs. He made sure we were fed and had a roof over our heads. We never doubted that he loved us. And you made sure we were safe and learned how to be good people." She sniffed. "The older I get, the more I realize how hard it was for you. Growing up, it was just…the way it was. Until I came to college, I didn't understand how different our lives were from everyone else's, how you never got a childhood and never learned to be carefree."

Hannah stared at her hand. Scratches marred her knuckles from crawling into the underbrush to hide from a sniper.

Her life was so different from her sister's.

Danger colored Hannah's life, coating every interaction with every person she talked to, until she wasn't sure what was real and what was a deep-seated pessimism that saw the world as a place of chaos and confusion with death around every corner.

The world was not a place that was stable or secure.

She'd grown up believing that. She'd worked hard to ensure that Zoe and Eli didn't.

Hannah swallowed the knot that insisted on sticking in her throat. "Zoe?"

"Yeah?"

"Did you marry Kevin because you were looking for a family? For that thing we didn't have growing up?"

"You're so cynical." Somehow, those words were said with affection. "I married Kevin because I love him and I want to spend the rest of my life with him. We didn't see a reason to wait, not when he has a job that will let me finish school. We've talked and prayed, and we opted to go ahead."

"Without telling me."

"You'd have fought, and I didn't want to fight."

Hannah's eyes slipped shut. "Am I really that hard-nosed?" So full of sharp edges and condemning words that her own sister couldn't confide in her?

"I love you, Hannah. Very much. And I say this with love."

Hannah tensed.

"You have a way of making everyone around you feel like they're ten years old. Like you have all the answers and the rest of us are behind the curve."

"You mean I make you feel stupid." Hadn't Gabe just said that to her?

Bowing her head, she could only cry out, *Oh, God... help me. Help me let go and love well.*

"I mean that you're bossy." Zoe was clueless to her sister's internal struggle. "Sis, you have to let go of controlling everything and everybody, because one day you're going to meet a guy and fall in love, and if you can't let him be a man, you're going to chase him away.

Men need to feel respected, or they run in the opposite direction."

Hannah's eyes popped open. Where was this coming from? "When did you get so wise?"

"I read a book." Zoe actually laughed. "Our preacher gave it to us when we first started discussing marriage. It's a general statement, and not true for everyone, but men tend to value respect first."

"And women?"

"Security." Zoe softened. "That's what you didn't have as a kid but that you gave to me and Eli. Maybe you need to find someone who makes you feel secure so you can let go of the need to control. You used to tell Eli and me that we could trust God for anything. That's some serious security right there. Trying to control everything is kind of a slap in His face, don't you think?"

If they'd had this conversation any other time, Hannah would have launched into anger with the force of a rocket leaving the atmosphere. But having seen Gabe's posture when he walked away, the words sank into her heart. The stark idea that she'd hurt him dug in and left indescribable pain in her chest.

She knew that he'd been bullied in his past, and she'd treated him just as badly recently, as though he was weak and helpless.

The thought that she'd wounded him made her nauseous. "Zo, I have to go, but I love you, and… I'm happy for you. We'll celebrate when I'm done with this op, okay?"

"Yeah, we will. And I love you too." Zoe disconnected the call.

Laying her phone on the bench, Hannah bent forward with her head between her knees, wrestling with rising pain. She'd hurt Gabe, and he deserved better.

Why did it feel like she was ripping her own insides into shreds though? Because she cared. She cared about how he felt and if he survived. She was terrified of losing him, of something happening to him, and not simply because she wanted to protect him.

She didn't want to live in a world without him. For nearly a decade, she'd wanted nothing more than to see him again, whether she'd admitted that to herself or not.

Because he'd found his way into her heart.

She needed to apologize. Needed to tell him that *he* was strong, and *she* was weak. That her reactions had nothing to do with him and everything to do with her.

She stood and brushed her hands down her thighs. No more dark-of-night apologies. She'd stand in front of Phillip and Thalia if she had to and admit—

The door opened and footsteps came down the stairs.

Gabe stepped into the room, his brow tight. "This is all wrong." He walked straight to her but stopped and stood just out of reach. "I'm not running away again. This is my house. My space." He stepped closer. "I'm not backing down out of concern for what you or anyone else thinks."

"You shouldn't." Her voice cracked like glass hitting the concrete floor. She forced herself to meet his eyes and not look away, although she desperately wanted to. Despite his words, there was pain in his expression. Pain she'd caused. "I'm sorry. More than you know. I never thought you were weak. I never should have implied that. I just… Pride makes me think I'm the strongest person in the room. But I'm not."

His head tilted slightly, but he crossed his arms, building a barrier between them. "What are you saying?"

She wasn't exactly sure, but she did know one thing. For the first time in her life, she was going to relinquish control by handing her heart to him.

FIFTEEN

Gabe tightened his grip on his biceps, his muscles tensing in his crossed arms. The longer Hannah stood in front of him, her lower lip between her teeth and her body radiating uncertainty, the more he wanted to stop being angry and to…to kiss her.

She'd apologized. What more did he want?

More than she'd ever given or would ever give him. He wanted her heart. Her life. She'd proven over and over that he'd have neither. She guarded them too closely.

But that couldn't stop every muscle in his body from wanting to close the space between them and to kiss her the way he should have last night. Holding nothing back. He couldn't. That would mean giving in. Letting her run the show. And he was done with that. Either they were equals or they were nothing.

Did she even realize there was so much more on the line than her investigation?

He backed away. He should leave, but not until she'd answered his question. "What are you saying, Hannah?"

Her eyes drifted shut and then slowly fluttered open again, pinning his gaze in a way that made him understand what those crazy songs were saying when they crooned about getting lost in someone.

He definitely had no idea where he was right now.

He barely noticed she'd stepped closer until her warm hand rested on his forearm.

She looked up at him and swallowed so hard he could hear it. "It was easier to act like you were weak than to tell you that…that I've loved you since the first time I met you."

"What?" The word escaped on a breath. He hadn't heard her right. He was so lost, and he'd clearly left his brain behind.

"You can do what you want with that information." Her fingers tightened on his arm as her voice grew husky. "You can crush me with it. Use it against me. Wreck my career because I've fallen for an asset. I—" Her words stuttered to an unintelligible stop, and she started to back away.

Gabe lost all of his willpower. As her hand fell from his arm, he reached for it and caught her wrist, drew her gently to him. She opened her fingers against his chest, looking up at him as though she was waiting for him to decide what happened next.

But no. He wouldn't take anything. They would share. He laid his free hand flat against her cheek, letting his thumb trail across her lower lip in a silent question.

She answered by easing up on tiptoe and meeting him halfway.

This kiss was so much different than their first. On the swing, he'd been grad-school Gabe kissing grad-school Hannah the way he'd always longed to.

But this? This was grown-up Gabe kissing the woman he was most definitely in love with.

The one who'd confessed she loved him.

This was something he'd never experienced before. A sharing. A sense of being known, inside and out, good and bad, weak and strong. He loved this woman with everything he had.

For the first time, he knew she loved him in return. She'd handed him her heart, the thing he'd wanted most. She'd surrendered the deepest parts of her to do with as he wished, trusting him, sharing with him... *You can crush me with it. Use it against me. Wreck my career because I've fallen for an asset.*

The words tickled the back of his brain, stealing the tenderness of the moment, pulling him out of their kiss. *I've loved you since the first time I met you... An asset. An asset.*

He slipped away from her, dropping her hand and studying her face. Words and actions and memories locked into place.

How had he missed it before?

"Gabe?" The hesitancy in her voice was all he needed to turn the last key and to set the lock. She hadn't meant to say that much, to tip her hand and tell him the whole truth.

She had fallen in love with him before, he didn't doubt it. But the thing that had kept them apart *then* muscled its way between them *now.*

The affection in her eyes was hooded. She knew he'd heard. "Gabe, it's not—"

He held a hand up between them. Whatever she had to say, he wasn't ready to hear it. "You used me." The picture came into sharper focus. "You used me to get to Trevor. That's why..." The words trailed off. He couldn't even speak them. That's why she'd been so quick to abandon their friendship for Trevor's overtures. Why she'd disappeared when Trevor was arrested.

The job was over. She'd moved on to the next one. She'd do the same again.

Her expression was resigned. She didn't reach for him. It was as though she'd expected him to back away. "I couldn't stay then, not with the investigation ongoing. Even now, it's tricky with Trevor threatening an appeal. You never should have found out. I never should have—"

"You never should have told me?" Gabe dragged his hand down his face. "Were you ever going to tell me?"

"When I could."

"What about now?" He waved a hand between them. "Is any of this real, or are you still digging for evidence?"

She winced. "It was real then, and it's even more real now." There was no begging, just truth. Heartbroken truth. "I had to walk away then or compromise the investigation and my entire career."

He believed her, but he couldn't fully comprehend it. This was the latest twist in a roller coaster he'd never asked to ride. What he needed was time with Hannah that wasn't constantly interrupted by gunfire and chaos.

No. What he needed was time away to think. To process. To decide if he wanted to make a life change that included Hannah and the job with her team. He needed time to pray, and he knew just where to go. The one place that felt like home. "I'm going to the Mathisons'."

Her head jerked up, and she stared at him before nodding once. The gesture spoke of a confidence that her eyes didn't reflect. "I understand. But leave your phone here. I don't want Leigh or anyone else to be able to track you."

Gabe tapped the side of the phone for a second before laying it on the weight bench. The disconnect made him antsy, but she was right. Leigh had admitted to tracking him before.

"I'll send Phillip with you."

No. He wanted to go alone. But one look at the set of her jaw said that arguing would be fruitless. "Fine. You can stay here as long as you need. I just—"

Her ringing phone sliced through his words. *Of course.*

Two rings passed as she watched him, seeming to wait for him to speak. When he didn't, she pulled the phone from her pocket and frowned at the screen before answering. "Austin."

Her eyes went wide and then narrowed as she listened. When she finally spoke, her voice was tight. "Text me the address." She listened some more before she ended the call, pocketed the phone and motioned for him to follow her.

She was three steps up the stairs before she explained herself. "That was Sadie Lawson."

Gabe practically missed the lowest step. "Why is she calling you?"

"Because—" Hannah glanced over her shoulder at him as she reached for the door "—she says she knows who's trying to kill you."

This was probably a colossal setup.

Hannah pulled into a parking space outside a bustling strip mall in Asheville and scanned her surroundings. Cars jammed the parking lot outside a grocery store that was hopping with Friday afternoon shoppers who were planning weekend meals and impulse buying snacks as though life was perfectly normal.

Meanwhile, she'd be shocked if she survived the next half hour. "See anything I should worry about?"

Thalia was stationed nearby, watching the parking lot. It had taken some convincing, but Gabe had agreed to stick with his plan to head to the Mathisons' home, far away from Sadie. There was no telling what the younger woman had planned.

"No evidence of snipers or anyone loitering. Looks clear to me." Thalia's voice came through in her ear.

Actually, nothing was clear, especially given the way things had been going with Gabe when Sadie called. She'd always known that the moment Gabe learned the truth would be a tipping point...

They were still teetering there.

Pulling her hands from the wheel, Hannah shook them and recentered herself. Personal business had no weight in this moment. If she got lost in her heart, someone could die.

Someone like Gabe.

"She's pulling in." Thalia spoke the words that solidified Hannah's professional resolve and set what was hopefully the end of this into motion.

An electric-blue Ford Mustang slid into the space beside hers. Sadie's vehicle. The one she'd said she'd be driving.

"I have her." Hannah spoke without moving her lips. The last thing she needed was for Sadie to figure out she was in communication with outside help.

After a moment's pause, Sadie exited her vehicle and shouldered a large handbag. She fingered the leather strap, her gaze darting around the parking lot before she skittered over to Hannah's SUV and climbed in as they'd planned.

Sadie Lawson didn't look like a hardened criminal.

Her eyes were so wide that Hannah could see the whites all around them. Her long brown hair was frizzed as though she'd been running her hands through it. She fidgeted in the seat as though fire ants crawled all over her.

No, this was not a criminal mastermind, nor was it the woman who had talked a big game at the gala. This was a terrified young woman who was clearly in over her head.

Hannah gave her a moment to settle. She avoided looking directly at Sadie, opting to focus on the front window while keeping watch out the corner of her eye.

"You look scared." She made the observation aloud, more for Thalia than to soothe Sadie.

"You would be too if you were me." The mumbled words bounced on a tremor. "He's not going to like that I met with you. He's not going to like any of this." She lunged for the door. "I should go."

Hannah grabbed Sadie's biceps before she could bolt and pulled her gently back into the seat. "If you're afraid of someone, we can protect you."

Sadie's muscles didn't relax, though she did release the door handle. "In the movies, this would be the place where I say that no one can protect me." Her chuckle was bitter. "Sad thing is, that might be true."

Now really wasn't the time to let Sadie dialogue about her fears or waffle about her reasons for being here. They were exposed in the parking lot, although no one else seemed to be paying them any attention. The sooner Sadie spoke, the sooner they could get her to safety and save Gabe. "Why did you call me?"

It almost seemed Sadie had forgotten their prior contact. Her head swung toward Hannah, and she blinked like someone waking from a deep sleep. When her expression cleared, it was set with new resolve, almost as though her personality had changed from terrified victim to calculated aggressor. But her demeanor didn't speak of anger. It spoke of determination.

Hauling her designer purse onto her lap, Sadie rested both hands on it and stared at the expensive leather, eventually exhaling a long sigh. "I'm assuming by now that you've taken a dive into NJN. Our finances and the like."

Hannah said nothing. The less she spoke, the more likely that Sadie would say something helpful.

She ran her finger along a seam in the leather. "When I was asked straight out of law school to chair the board, I was floored. Flattered. Excited. It's a nonprofit, but it pays well, and I thought I'd get to help people." Her gaze darted to Hannah and then away. "Problem is, the organization is nothing like they say it is."

"Because someone is embezzling big-time." Forget being silent, she had to move this along. "Who?" It was definitely the same person Sadie feared.

"So you do know."

"You pull in a lot of money, and Trevor Haskell's case was a genius way to catapult the NJN into the national spotlight. If I had to guess, you raked in a jackpot the other night at that gala of yours."

"You're right." Sadie finally lifted her chin and faced Hannah. "I thought they saw something in me, but what they saw was a young, untested lawyer who could be easily manipulated. A puppet. A…" Her eyes shone with unshed tears. "A pretty face to draw in donors. To gain sympathy for the cause." Shaking her head, Sadie looked down at her purse. "I haven't helped anyone. All of those cases the other night? Slam dunks. They were going to get out on parole or get retrials anyway.

We simply stepped in at the last minute and took the credit. They said it was a way to build a name for ourselves so we could help more people in the long run, but I saw how much we brought in the other night. I also saw what we reported. The numbers were very different. Tens of thousands of dollars different."

"I'm not surprised."

"Not by that, but maybe by this." Sadie unclipped a thumb drive from the side of her purse and passed it to Hannah. "NJN has a shadow board. They aren't public. They control what actually happens in the organization, and they take in the money. The public board? The one you see on the website and at the galas? They have no idea someone else is acting behind the scenes."

"How did you find out?"

"I followed the money and found that information buried in a handwritten file. There are photos on this thumb drive of the off-line books. They don't want to be found, but they don't trust one another not to cheat each other, if that makes sense. So they do everything aboveboard in their secret group."

The earpiece crackled. "This is all really interesting. I mean *really* interesting. But what does this have to do with Gabe? She needs to speed this up. I don't like how long this is taking."

Hannah ignored Thalia's sarcasm but not her warning. Thalia often had a good sense of impending danger. "Sadie, I'm going to ask you again, why did you call me?"

With a deep breath, Sadie shoved her hand into her bag so quickly that Hannah reached for her pistol. But the younger woman didn't produce a weapon. She withdrew two canvas books and held them out to Hannah. "You'll be interested in these."

"These are Dr. Donovan Mathison's journals." Hannah took them and laid them in her lap. "How did you get them?" Was she the mysterious buyer Hunter had mentioned?

"Trevor Haskell."

"What?" Thalia's voice rattled her eardrum.

Hannah tried not to flinch. Her people really needed to keep their thoughts to themselves. "Trevor had them?" If this was true, then he'd lied to them at the prison. Hunter Mathison had lied to them in Gatlinburg.

Or Sadie Lawson was lying right now.

"If I tell you everything, can you protect me?" Sadie's gaze was direct and sincere, but the lines creasing her forehead aged her, made her look older than her young years. "I want this to end, but if I talk, it's going to take money out of pockets. People don't like that."

There wasn't a lot that Hannah could promise without talking to people higher than her, but she could tell the truth. "I will do my very best. That's all I can say."

Sadie chewed her lower lip and stared at her clasped hands. "It's enough."

"We're listening." Thalia reminded Hannah she was there and could back up her story if Sadie recanted later.

"Go ahead." Really, this did need to move along. Hannah grabbed her phone. "If it's okay with you, I'm going to record this."

"I understand." Sadie nodded. "I should ask for a lawyer and a thousand other things. I know this, but I'm just…" She sniffed back tears. "Trevor Haskell contacted me. He'd received the journals anonymously in the mail with a note to let NJN help him. He was furious about Gabe Buchanan's involvement in getting him arrested. The public board saw the chance to go national by taking on a high-profile case like Trevor's, so they agreed. That should have been enough. But then the shadow board saw a payday in the program that's mentioned in the journals and suggested we sue to get the rights to it once Trevor has been retried and set free."

"So Trevor isn't involved?"

"Not at first. But he started calling me. He started to focus on revenge. Said he'd figured out where the journals came from and would help the guy take Gabe down. He started passing info to the guy through me."

"And that information is protected under attorney-client privilege." Which explained how Trevor could hack Gabe from prison. He had a puppet outside.

Sadie nodded. "I said I wanted out. I wanted to give up my job and to walk away. But Trevor's outside man said he'd kill me if I did. So I..." Sadie tipped her head toward the journals in Hannah's lap. "I took them from the safe at NJN. I don't know what good it will do for you to have them, but it has to be proof of something. Of them being illegally obtained, possibly? If you can prove that, it may render them inadmissible as evidence against Gabe or for Trevor. But I want out. Right now. However that looks."

"Okay. I can get you somewhere safe for now, then we'll see what we can do." Hannah reached down and started her SUV. She could take Sadie to headquarters while they sorted this out. Maybe she would tell them more once she felt secure. "But who is Trevor's man on the outside?"

"Hunter Mathison." Sadie's eyebrows drew together as though just saying his name brought on a tremor of fear. "His mother heads up the shadow board as a way for her and two of her fellow corporate lawyers to pad their accounts."

No. Hannah threw the SUV into Reverse. The tires

spit gravel as she executed a U-turn and roared out of the parking lot. "Thalia!"

"Calling Phillip now. And I'm right behind you."

As Sadie buckled her seat belt and gripped the handle above the door, Hannah prayed like never before.

Because Gabe wasn't just in the lion's den... He was in the mouth of the lion.

SIXTEEN

Gabe stared out the window of the Mathisons' guest room in the Blue Ridge Mountains, which were hazy in the late-day light. He scrubbed his hand on the top of his head and sank into a chair in the small sitting area that faced the floor-to-ceiling windows.

It had been amazing of Mrs. Mathison to let him crash here and to accommodate Phillip as well. Maybe he could settle his spirit.

So far, he was even more keyed up. He should have stayed by Hannah's side so that Phillip could've been involved with the meet between Hannah and Sadie. If he'd been more focused on helping her, Hannah would have had two more sets of eyes on her, two more people to protect her.

Instead, Gabe was hiding in a guest room, all up in his feelings, while Phillip was downstairs with Jeanette, going over the home's security system.

He didn't even know why he'd wanted to walk away in the first place. And the fact that he didn't know was messing with his head. Everything Hannah had done since her return spoke to her feelings being real. Could he fault her for doing her job years earlier?

Gabe groaned. Maybe he should go downstairs and

see if there was something he could do. Anything had to be better than moping while his thoughts ran wild.

He shoved up on the arms of the chair as a flash of sunlight caught the windshield of a vehicle. A red Chevy Equinox rounded the curve in the driveway, climbing toward the house.

Gabe stepped to the window and looked down at the SUV disappearing on the garage side of the house. Something about it tugged at a memory. He leaned closer to the glass, trying to catch a glimpse of the driver, though the vehicle was out of sight.

Phillip's voice echoed in his head. *One vehicle out-side around the back. Late 2010s Chevy SUV. Red.*

With a start, Gabe backed away from the window. That vehicle had been behind Hunter Mathison's cabin in Gatlinburg. Either Gabe's appearance at the cabin had incited a wave of guilt in the man...or bad things were about to happen.

He needed to call Hannah.

Reaching for his hip pocket, he stopped. No phone. He'd left it at the house as requested.

Why did he have to be such a rule follower?

Okay, he'd find Phillip. He should be in the butler's pantry, where Mrs. Mathison had said the security mon-itors were set up.

He needed to be stealthy though. If Hunter was up to no good, Gabe didn't want to be seen. The main stairs were out of the question, since they curved down to a foyer in full view of the main entrance, dining room and living room. There was a back flight of stairs that led into the kitchen, accessible by a door at the end of the hall.

At the bedroom threshold, he paused to listen. The hallway was silent, so he eased the door open and scanned the area. When he was certain he was alone, he slipped out and headed toward the rear of the house. Hopefully, he wouldn't show up on any cameras, or if he did, the only person to see him would be Phillip.

Voices from the foyer stopped him before he'd taken more than a few steps.

Jeanette Mathison was speaking, her tone edged with a sharpness Gabe had never heard before.

He tossed aside his mission to find Phillip. If Hunter had gotten into the house and was in a heated confrontation with his mother, Gabe had to help her. He crept toward the main stairs.

Hunter's voice drifted to him, icy and pointed. "What else did you want me to do?"

"Not come here." Jeanette snapped at him and then lowered her voice. "You should have stayed away."

Wait. This didn't sound like a surprise reunion. Backing against the wall, Gabe inched closer to the main staircase.

Hunter's next outburst ricocheted off the walls. "I didn't have a choice. Sadie found the journals. She took them to that agent. If you'd answer my calls, you'd know that."

"*That agent* wouldn't even know the journals existed if you hadn't decided you could make a quick buck off the government. You and Trevor were supposed to make it look like he received them anonymously. The payoff would have been much bigger than some little grant if you'd have let Trevor's lawsuit pay out. He'd have money from Gabe, money from the prison system and control of the software Gabe developed with your father. There's more money in that program than you can imagine. It belongs to you, because your father helped develop it. Gabe would have nothing if it wasn't for that. It'll be enough to pay off your father's debts for all of his pet inventions and to get you the help you need." There was a thread of desperation in the words.

Every ounce of air squeezed out of Gabe's chest. What was he hearing?

"If Gabe hasn't destroyed it already."

"He confirmed a copy exists. Frankly, at this point, he's nearly frightened enough to turn over the software without a nasty lawsuit. You've managed to convince him someone wants him dead. One more push, and he might have handed the whole thing off just to make it stop. He came here, didn't he? Given a day or two, he'd have confided the location to me, and we could have fixed everything."

Slumping against the wall, Gabe forced his mouth to remain closed. He'd been conned by a woman he'd thought loved him like family. Someone he'd trusted.

She must have found the notes in her husband's journals. She was smart enough to know the value of that software. If she was in financial trouble and was motivated to help her son get free of addiction...

She might be capable of anything.

Pressing his spine deeper into the wall, Gabe wrestled thoughts and emotions spinning so fast that the space around him might whirl as well.

Okay. He pulled in a deep breath and straightened, easing away from the stairs. *This is nothing but dealing with a bully. You know how to do this.*

But the bully had never been so close.

He had to find Phillip. It was chilling that the Mathisons weren't afraid Phillip would overhear them. He didn't think Jeanette was capable of harming anyone, but she hadn't hesitated to put him in harm's way in order to get him where she wanted him.

At the end of the hallway, he made his way down the back stairs into the well-lit, airy kitchen. The room was painted a pale yellow with white cabinets. Some had glass fronts and held the china Mrs. Mathison had once told him had belonged to her grandmother.

Gabe swallowed the emotion that fond memories threatened to bring up. He had to stay out of the past and in this twisted present.

Sticking close to the counter, he made his way around the island where Jeanette had cooked countless meals for him. The butler's pantry door was shut, but he eased it open and slipped inside. No Phillip. No security system.

It was getting harder not to panic.

At the back of the pantry, the door that led to a smaller food storage area was also closed. No sound came from the other side.

Gabe's stomach tightened. If Jeanette had lied about so much, she'd likely done something to Phillip. Heart pounding, Gabe pushed the door open and stepped inside the smaller room.

Phillip was slumped in the corner.

Dropping to his knees, Gabe felt for a pulse. It was there, though it was slow. He had no marks on him, no blood. She must have dosed him with something. He'd heard her offer Phillip a snack earlier.

The fact that the agent was still alive spoke volumes. The Mathisons weren't yet prepared to use deadly force.

It had better stay that way.

He scanned the room, searching for a phone, and then paused. There were no monitors. No security system. No nothing.

Jeanette had lied. Had she really thought no one would find out?

Gabe needed Phillip's cell. He'd call Hannah and the police.

Pulling the cell from Phillip's pocket, he spotted the pistol still in its holster. Jeanette must have assumed that whatever she'd dosed Phillip with was going to last a while, or she'd have disarmed him. Either that, or she'd panicked.

Gabe hesitated and then slipped the holster from Phillip's waistband and into his. He pulled his shirt down over it. He had no idea what he'd do with a gun, but something about being armed made him feel less vulnerable.

Rocking back onto his heels, he pressed the phone screen. It lit up, listing a dozen missed calls in the past ten minutes, all from Hannah. He pressed one.

The phone was locked and useless without a pass code. No one on the team used touch or Face ID.

Great.

Gabe glanced at the door and then the screen, willing Hannah to call again.

Or… He could make an emergency call even with the phone locked. He was pressing the key sequence when voices entered the kitchen.

"Where's Gabe now?" Hunter sounded urgent.

"Upstairs in the guest room. But this wasn't what we talked about." Jeanette's voice was frantic. "You can't take this too far. We never discussed this."

"Is Dad's gun still in the pantry?"

Gabe froze. If either of them walked in now, this would be over in an instant.

"Hunter, no."

"Look, we tried it your way, and now we have no other choice." Footsteps drew near. "Sadie has gone to that federal agent. We're implicated now. It's time to run, and we're taking Gabe with us. He'll lead us to his software and then—"

"You're not killing him."

"I'm not?" Hunter's voice rose to a dangerous level. "It's him or me at this point, *Mother*. Choose your favorite *son*."

The silence stretched so long Gabe wondered if they'd left. Finally, Jeanette spoke. "Your father's pistol is in my nightstand. I'll—"

The doorbell ended whatever her next plans were, though her words had already shattered Gabe's heart.

He'd been betrayed, but he would have to deal with that later. He strained to listen, praying that salvation stood on the front porch.

Hunter cursed. "I'll get the gun. You get rid of whoever that is…and then we'll end this once and for all."

Hannah pressed the doorbell again. This was taking too long, and she'd left Sadie handcuffed to her steering wheel.

The situation was not ideal.

"I'm in position. Can't see anyone." Thalia's voice was low in her ear. The other agent had crept to the back of the house. "No sign of Phillip or Gabe. Phillip's car and Hunter's SUV are here."

Hannah winced. "ETA on local LEOs?"

"Ten to fifteen." Thalia had phoned the Buncombe County sheriff on their race to the house, but given the remote location and the need to assemble a response team, help was going to take time.

Footsteps echoed inside the house, drawing near to the door. *Finally.*

Hannah rested her hand on her pistol grip. "I've got movement."

The door eased open, and an older woman with perfectly styled short gray hair, wearing jeans and a black sweater peered out. "Can I help you?" Heavy worry lines creased her forehead, and she glanced over her shoulder.

Yep. Something was definitely up in the Mathison house. With her free hand, Hannah held out her credentials. "I'm Chief Warrant Officer Hannah Austin with US Army special investigations. May I come in?"

"Army? I'm sorry. What does the Army want with me?"

Was she seriously going to play dumb? "Ma'am, I already know that Gabe Buchanan and one of my agents are onsite. May I come in, please?" She punched the words, packing them with every ounce of her authority.

"Not without a warrant."

Pressing her lips together, Hannah nodded slowly. Lawyers knew how to lawyer. She'd expected it.

Well, she knew how to lawyer too. "I have probable cause."

Jeanette Mathison's right eyebrow arched.

"Produce my agent and Gabe Buchanan. Show me they're safe. Otherwise, step aside and—"

A gunshot pinged off the column behind her.

Hannah dove for the door, slamming it behind her as she drew her weapon. "Where did that come from?" The exclamation was half shock and half query to Thalia.

Jeanette Mathison backed against the wall as Thalia yelled in Hannah's earpiece. "Circling to the front."

Pushing back the curtain, Hannah tried to judge the angle of the bullet. It had come from above and to the right.

From upstairs.

Whoever had fired that weapon wanted her in the

house. "Hunter's inside." And boy, was he living up to his name.

She spun toward the stairs, keeping one eye on Jeanette and one on the landing above the foyer. "Where's Hunter?"

"My son hasn't been here in—"

"Don't. His car is in the drive." She aimed her weapon upward and started toward the sweeping, curved staircase, sticking close to the wall. "Stay here."

Her heart pounded and adrenaline hit her in the gut. Why hadn't Gabe appeared? Where was Phillip?

As she reached the bottom of the stairs, a shadow moved at the top. A bullet skipped across the marble floor by her feet as a shot cracked.

Jumping backward, Hannah ducked around the corner and focused on the top of the stairs. "Hunter Mathison! This is Army chief warrant officer Hannah Austin! Put down—"

A force slammed into her from the side. Her head crashed into the wall, jarring her neck and filling her vision with stars. Her gun clattered to the ground, and the world went dark.

SEVENTEEN

Gabe stopped at the swinging door between the kitchen and the dining room. Why had Hannah stopped yelling midsentence? He hadn't heard another gunshot.

Yet something had clearly happened to her.

The world seemed to recede until all that existed was a thin line of sight directly in front of him. Even sound narrowed into a tunnel.

He could not let her die. There was no more thinking about this. He loved her. Always had. He'd do what it took to save her life.

Even if it meant losing his.

Gabe held Phillip's gun in both hands until his fingers ached. It felt foreign. Terrifying. Life and death in his grip.

He had to save Hannah, and he had to survive. If he was hurt saving her, Hannah would live with that guilt forever.

It was a chance he'd have to take.

Pulling in a deep breath, he opened the door an inch, the gun aimed at the floor. On the other side of the dining room, in the two-story foyer, Jeanette rose and scrambled backward, eyes wide with panic.

"I told you no killing in this house, Hunter! We'll never get away from this now."

Gabe froze, his muscles refusing to take another step. *No.* Hannah couldn't be dead.

Hunter stalked down the stairs, pistol in hand, focused on his mother. "Calm down. You knocked her out. She's still breathing."

Slowly exhaling a sigh of relief, Gabe sagged against the door frame. Hannah was safe for the next few seconds at least. He had time. Not a lot of time, but something.

Help had to get here soon.

Where was Thalia? She'd been with Hannah for the meeting with Sadie, which meant she should be close now. The sound of a gunshot should have drawn her into the fray...but it hadn't.

With Phillip unconscious and Thalia MIA, Gabe was the only one who could rescue Hannah. He'd told her he could handle this, that he wanted to get out from behind a screen and help in the real world.

Had he meant it?

No. Now it was clear that he'd been angry...and he'd been trying to be someone he wasn't.

It wasn't as though he had a choice now though. *God, help me.*

Hunter and his mother were focused on Hannah, their backs to him. Gabe slipped through the swinging door and let it catch on his foot, closing it gently. He'd have to cross the dining room, keeping close to the wall. With the open floor plan, there was no concealment. If either of the Mathisons turned, he'd be dead in their sights.

Gabe struggled to regulate his breathing, in and out, slowly, quietly.

He eased along the wall as Hunter and his mother stared at the figure slumped on the floor.

It took all he had not to fixate on Hannah's unmoving body. *Lord, save her.*

"It's all over anyway. If she's here, she's probably called the cops as well." Hunter glared at his mother with what might have been disdain if the expression hadn't been blended with panic. "New plan. If we take out everyone who can point the finger at us, we get away with it. Sadie is probably close. We kill both agents and Gabe, shoot Sadie with one of their guns, then put this gun in Sadie's hands and claim it was all her, that she stormed in demanding a payout or something. Then we both get out of here free."

"That will never work."

Listen to your mother, Hunter.

Maybe she'd stall her son. Get him thinking. Maybe they'd both simply bolt. After all, they were running out of time and options.

But Hunter simply ignored his mother. He raised the pistol and aimed it at Hannah.

At the window beside the door, a shadow moved. It had to be Thalia. She'd never get inside in time.

Phillip's gun was suddenly too heavy in Gabe's hands. Could he do it? Pull the trigger? Did he have a choice? He raised the pistol…and fired.

Hannah sat on the second step of the Mathisons' main staircase and stared at the bullet hole in the thick cream-colored wallpaper. Her head throbbed with each heartbeat, and every muscle in her body ached, but she was alive.

Thanks to Gabe.

The shot he'd fired had given Thalia the distraction she needed to kick in the front door and take Hunter down before he could fire a bullet into Hannah's head. Now Hunter and Jeanette Mathison were handcuffed in the back seat of two Buncombe County sheriff deputies' SUVs, awaiting transport. Sadie was in a third. She had a lot of explaining to do to the authorities.

It was finally over.

Thalia walked through the door, which still hung open from her forced entry, and settled onto the step beside Hannah. "Got two ambulances on the way."

She knew what that meant. One for Phillip. One for her. "How is he?"

"He's with a deputy who's a former paramedic. He's awake now. There's a prescription bottle on the counter near the kitchen sink. I didn't stop to look, but I'm guessing it's a sleep aid."

That would make sense. "So Jeanette had this planned all along?"

"Not murder but scaring Gabe into turning over the software. My guess is that when Gabe showed up with a bodyguard, she grabbed the first thing she had handy to keep the threat at bay, which was her own prescription. Lawyer that she is, she's silent. But Hunter? He's in the back of that patrol vehicle singing like he's up for a golden ticket to Hollywood on a reality TV show."

Figured. Tough guys often fell the fastest.

Hannah glanced at the hole in the wall again. "Where's Gabe?"

"Giving a statement to the sheriff and turning over the gun. When I saw him a second ago, he was talking and edging this way at the same time. He should be here any—"

"Hannah?" Right on cue, Gabe rushed through the door, finding her gaze immediately.

"—any second." Thalia stood and pointed at the spot on the stairs that she'd vacated next to Hannah. "I'll see how it's going with Phillip."

To be honest, it was shocking she wasn't already at his side. Those two were close. She'd seen more than one set of partners couple up over the years, though Phillip and Thalia were so different—

Gabe settled onto the step beside her and effectively halted her thoughts about anyone else. He was here, and he was safe. There was nothing more Hannah needed.

It was also what she'd almost lost.

She exhaled slowly. "When I didn't see you earlier, I thought…" It was the first time she'd let herself get lost in the "what might have been."

And those "might haves" terrified her.

"Back at ya." He leaned his shoulder against hers and stared across the foyer at a painting of the mountains at sunrise. "Seeing you on the floor, not moving…" He shook his head, his forehead creased. "I've had a lot of bad moments in my life, but that one?" When he turned toward her, he was close. Too close.

The intensity in his gaze was something she hadn't been prepared for.

She looked away, up at the bullet hole. Her head ached, but so did her heart. Did she dare act on what she was feeling? Because she knew for certain now what she'd always suspected… She loved this man. But loving him would change everything for her. For them. She couldn't command a team with him on it. She'd have to give up control of her life, let someone else in. Worry about someone else.

Could she do that?

She cleared her throat. "We need to work on your aim. Your shot was really high."

Gabe chuckled. "I wasn't trying to hit him. I saw Thalia through the window. I just wanted to slow him down before..." Gabe's exhale was loud. "If he'd killed you—"

"You'd have felt guilty for the rest of your life." She could understand that. She'd felt the same thing.

"No. I'd have died too." He reached over and laid one finger on her chin, gently turning her face toward him. "I'm pretty sure I've loved you since the first time you walked into the coffee shop. And I'm pretty sure what I felt then was nothing like this. My mistake then was not telling you because I was afraid you'd reject me. I won't make that mistake again."

Her eyes went wide. He was saying it. Saying what his actions had already spoken. When he'd walked away earlier, she'd been convinced she'd never hear the words, yet here they were.

"I love you, Hannah Austin. Every ounce of you. Even the control freak that's going to drive me positively batty at some point and probably make us fight more than we should. But I'll deal with it." He tilted his hand and traced her lower lip with his thumb. "I'll deal with all of it." His voice dropped so low she could barely hear it.

She scanned his eyes, half-afraid to speak after the rattle to her head. But she knew this wasn't a possible concussion making her heart race. It was the man in front of her. "My mistake was walking away from you nine years ago without telling you the truth. I've thought of you every day since then. And when I think of the time we've lost..." She leaned forward. This time when she kissed him, it would be freely, with everything in her.

But his grip on her chin tightened, even as the corner of his mouth lifted. "Not until you say it."

She arched an eyebrow. He was holding off on her kiss?

He matched her expression. "Say it."

Understanding flowed through her head like light rushing over the mountains at sunrise. Just like her, he needed to hear the words. Needed the assurance that she meant it. That she wouldn't disappear again. That she wanted to be his.

Dipping her head until her forehead rested against his, she closed her eyes. "I love you. It's something I can't control, and it terrifies me, but I do. And I'll—"

She never got to finish the sentence. He closed the gap between them and kissed her gently, tenderly, as though he was afraid of hurting her.

Given that she likely had a concussion, he probably should be.

For the first time in her life, she let go of control. She let Gabe take the lead, let him know exactly how she felt with no fences, no walls, nothing to guard herself from pain.

She let herself be free.

When he pulled away, he swept her hair from her face, following the motion with his gaze before he met her eyes again. "I'm not joining your team."

The stark statement splashed her emotions like frigid rain. "What?"

His finger trailed down her cheek, leaving warmth behind. Something in his expression said he didn't really want to talk about work, but that he needed to say this.

Hannah dug her teeth into her lip, trying to focus on his words over his touch. It wasn't easy.

"I thought I needed to prove myself. To be in the field and fight with my hands to be the man you need."

Her heart squeezed. She loved him just like he was. He didn't need to perform for her. "I never meant to make you feel—"

"I put that pressure on myself. That's on me. But I'm happy, Hannah. I'm happy with my business, and I'm happy profiling job candidates. I'm staying where I am." He pressed a kiss to her forehead. "You chase the bad guys. I'll make sure none of them land jobs where they can cause harm."

"Deal." As much as she knew giving up control was what God was asking of her, she was also grateful she wouldn't have to worry about Gabe undercover on a team. Today had been hard enough. "Now what?"

"Now you take a ride in the ambulance. And after that…" He pulled away and smiled in a way she'd never seen before.

It was a smile that shot straight though her. "After that?" Her voice broke. Yeah, her emotions were giving her away.

"Well, you talked about lost time…"

She could only nod. He'd stolen her ability to speak.

"How about you shock your brother and sister and do the last thing they expect?"

The mischief in his gaze melted into something different. Something she wanted to dive into for the rest of her life. Him. "Like marry you as soon as the hospital clears me?"

"Something like that." Gabe's smile was electric.

"I can do that."

This time, when she kissed him, she handed him her heart…and the rest of her life.

* * * * *

If you enjoyed this story, please look for these other books by Jodie Bailey:

Blown Cover
Witness in Peril
Captured at Christmas

Dear Reader

Wounds take time to heal. The deeper I dove into Gabe and Hannah's story, the more I realized how true that is. Gabe was a particularly complex character to write, as he was suffering from a past that made him feel inferior and weak. Wounds inflicted on him as a kid had left scars…and they were still painful. He spent his life trying to fit into a mold that wasn't made for him. And the more I got to know him, the more I recognized that.

That's why, in the end, Gabe figured out that he liked himself and his life exactly the way he was already living it. He didn't need to be someone else. He simply needed to be the Gabe that God created him to be. To embrace the honor of fighting battles in an unconventional way that didn't involve him becoming a "tough guy" to impress himself or anyone else.

Gabe reminded me that God created each of us with a purpose and a personality that is uniquely ours. We don't have to fit someone else's mold. Scars and all, we are who we are, and our lives are shaped in a way that proves we have been "fearfully and wonderfully made."

I hope you know that God has created you to be someone special. That He uses the events in our lives to shape who we become. And that we, in turn, use the sum total of our God-created selves and our experiences to serve Him and to help others as only we can.

Thanks for hanging out with me—and with Gabe and Hannah. Drop by jodiebailey.com if you'd like to say hi! I look forward to more on-page adventures soon!

Jodie Bailey

COMING NEXT MONTH FROM
Love Inspired Suspense

LOOK FOR THESE AND OTHER LOVE INSPIRED BOOKS WHEREVER BOOKS ARE SOLD, INCLUDING MOST BOOKSTORES, SUPERMARKETS, DISCOUNT STORES AND DRUGSTORES.

LISCNM0223

Get 4 FREE REWARDS!

We'll send you 2 FREE Books <u>plus</u> 2 FREE Mystery Gifts.

FREE
Value Over
$20

Both the **Love Inspired®** and **Love Inspired® Suspense** series feature compelling novels filled with inspirational romance, faith, forgiveness and hope.

YES! Please send me 2 FREE novels from the Love Inspired or Love Inspired Suspense series and my 2 FREE gifts (gifts are worth about $10 retail). After receiving them, if I don't wish to receive any more books, I can return the shipping statement marked "cancel." If I don't cancel, I will receive 6 brand-new Love Inspired Larger-Print books or Love Inspired Suspense Larger-Print books every month and be billed just $6.49 each in the U.S. or $6.74 each in Canada. That is a savings of at least 16% off the cover price. It's quite a bargain! Shipping and handling is just 50¢ per book in the U.S. and $1.25 per book in Canada.* I understand that accepting the 2 free books and gifts places me under no obligation to buy anything. I can always return a shipment and cancel at any time by calling the number below. The free books and gifts are mine to keep no matter what I decide.

Choose one: ☐ **Love Inspired**
Larger-Print
(122/322 IDN GRHK)

☐ **Love Inspired Suspense**
Larger-Print
(107/307 IDN GRHK)

Name (please print)

Address   Apt. #

City   State/Province   Zip/Postal Code

Email: Please check this box ☐ if you would like to receive newsletters and promotional emails from Harlequin Enterprises ULC and its affiliates. You can unsubscribe anytime.

Mail to the **Harlequin Reader Service:**
IN U.S.A.: P.O. Box 1341, Buffalo, NY 14240-8531
IN CANADA: P.O. Box 603, Fort Erie, Ontario L2A 5X3

Want to try 2 free books from another series? Call 1-800-873-8635 or visit www.ReaderService.com.

*Terms and prices subject to change without notice. Prices do not include sales taxes, which will be charged (if applicable) based on your state or country of residence. Canadian residents will be charged applicable taxes. Offer not valid in Quebec. This offer is limited to one order per household. Books received may not be as shown. Not valid for current subscribers to the Love Inspired or Love Inspired Suspense series. All orders subject to approval. Credit or debit balances in a customer's account(s) may be offset by any other outstanding balance owed by or to the customer. Please allow 4 to 6 weeks for delivery. Offer available while quantities last.

Your Privacy—Your information is being collected by Harlequin Enterprises ULC, operating as Harlequin Reader Service. For a complete summary of the information we collect, how we use this information and to whom it is disclosed, please visit our privacy notice located at corporate.harlequin.com/privacy-notice. From time to time we may also exchange your personal information with reputable third parties. If you wish to opt out of this sharing of your personal information, please visit readerservice.com/consumerchoice or call 1-800-873-8635. **Notice to California Residents**—Under California law, you have specific rights to control and access your data. For more information on these rights and how to exercise them, visit corporate.harlequin.com/california-privacy.

LIRLIS22R3

HARLEQUIN
PLUS

Try the best multimedia subscription service for romance readers like you!

Read, Watch and Play.

Experience the easiest way to get the romance content you crave.

Start your **FREE TRIAL** at
<u>www.harlequinplus.com/freetrial</u>.

HARPLUS0123